# COLT LIGHTNING

Jay McGraw was lucky to be fast on his feet when he chose the outlaw life instead of the gallows. Falsely accused of murder, he busted out of prison and headed for the hills with the posse right behind. At the McPherson ranch, a kind cowboy hid him and Jay's escape was good—for the moment.

But once he accepted a job there breaking mustangs, Jay discovered a lot more was involved, including cattle rustling, bloodthirsty feuds, ruthless outlaws, and Tombstone showdowns. Jay had to be fast to hold his own—that was why they called him 'Lightning.'

D0930966

# COLT LIGHTNING

## Tim Champlin

GUNSMOKE

This hardback edition 2002
by Chivers Press
by arrangement with
Golden West Literary Agency

ISBN 0 7540 8194 X

**British Library Cataloguing in Publication Data available.**

Printed and bound in Great Britain by
BOOKCRAFT, Midsomer Norton, Somerset

To the memory of my father, Dr. John B. Champlin (1909–1964).

He was one of several veterinarians employed by the U.S. Department of Agriculture who was sent to Mexico in 1949 to help that government stem an outbreak of foot-and-mouth disease. Their combined efforts were successful in preventing the spread of this very contagious disease to the cattle of the United States.

# CHAPTER 1

JAY MCGRAW knew his pursuers were still behind him and closing in fast. Even though he had not heard the crash of brush or the clattering of loose shale in the past few minutes, he knew they were still there and moving swiftly through the dense chaparral.

He scrambled the last few yards up to the top of the ridge and paused on trembling legs in the scant cover of a mesquite bush. Listening intently, he heard nothing but his own harsh breathing and felt the rapid pounding of his heart. Sweat stung his eyes and dripped from the end of his nose as his sides heaved in and out in great, sobbing gasps. He knew he was nearing the end of his endurance. He was a sprinter, not a long-distance runner, but he had run nearly flat-out for at least three miles, much of it uphill through thigh-high grass and thick stands of mesquite, cedar, juniper, and oak. He had kept to the heaviest cover, where horses could not follow.

A bloody spot stained the right knee of his torn Levi's where he had slipped and gone down on a rock-covered slope. But he was no more aware of it than he was of the many cuts and scratches on his arms and neck where the brush had whipped and stung him. He mopped his face with a soggy shirtsleeve, dropped to one knee, and leaned

1

both elbows on the other in a semi-resting position to get his breath. He spat cotton into the dry grass.

Thank God it wasn't the Apaches who were on his trail, he thought. It was bad enough having three white men and two Mexican-Pima half-breeds chasing him. But at least a long, tortured death did not await him if he were caught. Probably only a quick jerk of his neck at the end of a rope instead, he thought wryly.

The Pima half-breeds were mostly lazy, but, if promised a reward for his capture, they might get enthusiastic about the chase. It was only when employed as Army scouts that they often lost their taste for tracking—especially when the quarry was their ancient enemy, the wily and deadly Apache.

Following his break from the adobe jail at Washington Camp, Jay had borrowed the nearest horse and ridden, hell-bent and bareback, for the nearest and thickest woods and the steepest hills. He guessed that his pursuers had also abandoned their mounts, since they would otherwise have caught up with him by now. But no horse he had ever seen could follow where he led.

His breathing and heartbeat gradually began to steady down, though sweat still poured from his body. His pursuers must be tiring, heavy-booted and carrying rifles as they were. The sultry summer heat of these wooded Patagonia Mountains on the western side of the Huachucas, in southeastern Arizona Territory, had to be taking its toll on them, as it was on him. But they were not athletes, conditioned as he was, nor did they have the spur of desperation to urge them on.

Abruptly, the afternoon stillness was punctured by the rattle of small stones, followed by a muffled curse. Startled, Jay forced himself to his feet and stared intently down his backtrail, but could see nothing in the thick greenery. He estimated the sound to be no more than sixty yards away. He had been wise not to underestimate the endurance or persistence of his trackers.

2

Being careful where he stepped, he skirted a thick stand of cedar and glided swiftly and silently onward, continuing in a northwesterly direction. He loped smoothly around and through the dense growth, avoiding the underbrush wherever he could, keeping to the tall grass where his footfalls in the knee-high Apache moccasins were virtually silent. His brief rest had allowed him to catch his second wind, and he glided with long, ground-eating strides that came a little easier as he passed over the crest of the hill and started on a long, gradual descent. His feet were bruised inside the thick hide soles of the moccasins, his thirst was acute, and spiderwebs continually wrapped themselves around his face and head as he ran between closely spaced cedar trees.

Where was he going? The Mowry Mine lay somewhere ahead, but he didn't know exactly where.

Bought by a Lieutenant Sylvester Mowry in 1860, it had quickly developed into one of the richest mines in the territory, producing $1,000 a day in silver. In 1862, Mowry was arrested for allegedly supplying the Confederacy with lead from the mine for making bullets, and was imprisoned at Fort Yuma several months before the charges were dropped for lack of evidence. His confiscated mine was never returned to him. Even though he attempted to get it back through legal means, the government sold it at auction in 1864, and Mowry died a poor man a few years later in England.

The mine had played out, and the adobe buildings and smelter around it had been abandoned several years ago. Many of the empty buildings and mine shafts would provide good hiding places—if he could find them. He had passed them on the road to Washington Camp ten days ago, but all these hills and valleys looked alike to him. Maybe he should have headed south for the Mexican border, which was no more than a couple of miles from Washington Camp. But he doubted his pursuers would have stopped at the invisible international boundary, even if they knew where it was. He had to avoid all roads and trails. If the men after him got to the mining town of Harshaw, about four miles beyond Mowry, they could obtain mounts, and possibly pick up a few more men for a posse.

He loped along, his mind sorting out the possibilities, his lean, muscular body automatically moving like a well-lubricated machine. He had to put more distance between himself and his hunters before he considered stopping or holing up until dark. He knew that when the breakout occurred, just before noon, the men had taken after him without stopping to round up any tracking dogs. They probably thought they would have him recaptured quickly. None of them knew this would settle into a long, exhausting chase. Why hadn't they given up? Clay Dawson, the sheriff and leader of his pursuers, was a proud and stubborn man, Jay had discovered during his five days of confinement in the Washington Camp jail. He would view a breakout from his jail as a personal affront to his capabilities as a peace officer, and Jay suspected that Dawson would go to any lengths to recapture an escapee. His escape had been especially galling since he had tricked Dawson's nephew, Tige Taggert, into removing his shackles while he was being escorted to the outhouse. And it was Tige Jay had humiliated earlier at the footraces and wrestling matches during a field day celebration, collecting $300 in first-place prize money and an equal amount from side bets he had placed on himself. The local townsfolk of the small mining camp didn't take kindly to a stranger coming in and making fools of the local boys. So when Tige's girl had taken it into her head to sidle up to Jay, a fight had ensued. In the melee that followed, some drunken fool had pulled a gun. Jay, outnumbered, had jerked his own .38 Colt Lightning to defend himself, and a wild shot had hit and killed the twelve-year old son of a Mexican

4

miner. From the way the boy was hit, the shot could have come from any one of two or three guns, since a half-dozen men, including Jay, were throwing lead from behind wagons and horse troughs. But Jay had been jailed immediately by Sheriff Dawson, who had put a stop to further gunplay with a shotgun blast over their heads. Jay had argued, unsuccessfully, that it could have been another man who fired the fatal shot, since most of the bystanders had been diving for cover at the time and did not actually see it happen. The bullet had passed right through the boy and was not found, but Sheriff Dawson and the local storekeeper-undertaker, in the absence of any further experts, both concluded that the entry wound had been caused by a .38-caliber slug. And since he, Jay, had been the only one using that caliber gun, he was immediately guilty by process of elimination. Jay had not been allowed to view the body, so he could not decide if they were correct. In any event, it would have been his word against theirs. And there was no doubt about whose word would prevail. Even though Sheriff Dawson had tried to act the part of the professional lawman as he disarmed Jay, relieved him of his newly won $600, and led him to a cell, Jay had noted the look of smug satisfaction on his face. Fate had played into their hands, and this arrogant stranger was going to get what was coming to him. If Jay had harbored any doubts about his immediate future, the grin on Tige's face dispelled all guesswork.

"They're gonna stretch your neck for murder, boy!"

The lopsided grin on the face of the burly, young athlete was caused by a bruised and swollen mouth and cheek, the result of Jay's beating in the rough-and-tumble, no-holds-barred wrestling match.

Now, as he bounded downhill through the timber, Jay almost grinned at the thought of what Tige must be enduring. He would be held responsible for the escape. The only thing Jay regretted was that he had not been able to arm himself. There was simply no time. As it was, only his speed and agility had enabled him to flatten Tige with one punch and reach the horse that grazed a few yards beyond the outhouse before his jailer was up and trying to get a shot off at him.

He continued to run, letting his mind rove back over the details of his break. By concentrating on this event, he wasn't quite as aware of his tiring muscles and his burning thirst. He had no water, no weapon, and was only vaguely aware of where he was.

He had a fleeting wish that he could somehow vanish or shrink to the size of a mouse. Yet there was no time for regrets—regrets that he had ever come to the Arizona Territory from his small western Iowa town in the first place. Just staying alive in this territory for more than a year had proven to be an exciting daily challenge. But for a young man just turned twenty-three, it was still better than being bored to death as an apprentice brick mason in his father's company or driving a hay-baler in someone else's fields. He needed excitement, adventure. Yet, for Jay McGraw, adventure was one thing, sheer terror, quite another.

A rumble, like the noise from a loaded ore wagon, came to his ears, and he pulled up beside some fallen timber, his heart jumping at the sound. But it was only the distant grumbling of thunder. The sky, unnoticed until now, had darkened as huge thunderheads boiled up high to the north and west of him, black with columns of white clouds towering thousands of feet into the sky. He listened, but there was no sound of pursuit. They might be anywhere from a quarter mile to a mile behind him by now, he guessed. If they had lost sight and sound of him, they might even be going in the wrong direction. With no dogs or good Indian trackers, they would play hell finding him in this wilderness of wooded hills and ravines. If he could get far enough ahead, he might chance trying to hole up somewhere in a rocky cave or an abandoned mine shaft, which were numerous in these hills. The approaching rainstorm might be the only thing that would save him. A hard downpour would not only wash out any sign or scent of his passing, it would also provide him with a refreshing shower of much-needed water. If he could stay out of sight and keep moving until the storm broke, he might confuse his pursuers.

He started on down the long slope, eyes and ears alert to any possible danger. The mule deer in these mountains were probably gone to their shady dens to rest out the heat of midday. Even the birds seemed to have quieted in the blanket of sultry June heat. He spied no squirrels, rabbits, or small animals in his flight. All nature seemed to be taking a siesta, or was hushed into inactivity by the increasing darkness of the approaching storm.

He ran on at a steady pace for another several minutes before stopping again. He scanned the area for any sign of the buildings that would mark the abandoned Mowry Mine, but saw only the deepening black overcast.

A gentle breeze fanned the leaves of the trees around him, stirring the sluggish heat. Then it began to blow a little stronger, with a sound like rushing water, penetrating the thick growth to bring a blessed coolness to his overheated body. Thunder crashed, long and rumbling, and much closer.

Had he outdistanced his pursuers? Had they given up and turned back? Maybe the oncoming storm had finally discouraged them. There was no telegraph at Washington Camp, so Sheriff Dawson could not wire other towns in the southern Arizona Territory to be on the lookout for him. A messenger would have to be sent on horseback to the other mining towns or to a town with a telegraph.

As he jogged on at a slower pace, he wondered how badly they really wanted him. His jailing on a charge of murder to await trial had been more of an act of revenge than of justice, he thought. There was no way they could make a charge of murder stick. Jay McGraw had made some mistakes in his life but he was not a killer. Even the accusation that he could be responsible for the death of a boy not yet in his teens was intolerable to him. He had to escape those who had no interest in proving him innocent of the charges.

He loped across an open space in the trees on a long downslope covered with high, thin grass, savoring the wind that dried the sweat on his body. A rifle cracked somewhere to his left and a slug hummed past his ear. His heart jumped. He bounded in long, graceful leaps toward the tree line.

"There he goes, boys! Get that slippery sonuvabitch!"

He heard other shouts from farther away, and then two more quick shots as he lunged for cover. He snagged the toe of one moccasin in the limb of a downed dead cedar and pitched headlong, rolling over and back to his feet as nimble as a cat. But he had lost precious time. He saw Sheriff Dawson running clumsily across the clearing behind him, waving the others on with his rifle. They were barely fifty yards behind him. He was unarmed and exhausted. With a sinking heart he realized he had been run to earth.

# CHAPTER 2

**B**UT fear gave him a surge of adrenalin. He wasn't about to give up without a fight. He sprinted away, running blindly from the men behind him, across another small clearing and into a denser growth of mesquite. He could hear the report of guns and the zipping of bullets through the leaves over his head. His feet flew over the ground, hardly seeming to touch down as small branches whipped his face and shirt.

*Craack!*

A sudden, sizzling bolt of lightning split the huge snag of a dead oak standing on a promontory hardly two hundred yards away. The stab of lightning was followed immediately by an earsplitting crash of thunder, and then a smoky veil of rain swept across the hill and blotted out everything in a downpour. The cool water felt good on his body as it streamed down his hair and face and soaked his already-wet shirt and Levi's. He tasted salt on his lips.

He glanced back quickly. The dogged sheriff and his men were not in sight. Now, with the slope of the land starting upward again, this might be a good time to quit running in a straight line and take a hard right to maybe throw them off his trail. The rushing roar of the storm would mask any noise he made, as long as he could stay out of their line of sight. He dodged to his right and followed the steep hill down through a thick stand of juniper and scrub oak. A hundred yards of this and he was into the thick mesquite again. Then the growth thinned slightly. He ran through a few scattered junipers and suddenly burst out into a narrow, grassy valley, with buildings and a corral in the middle of it. He ran on a few steps out of his cover and stopped, his heart pounding. He rubbed a hand across his streaming face. Through the murky downpour of rain, the wooden buildings looked like black, irregular blocks in the middle of the wide field. He had to find cover. Should he duck back into the woods, or should he make a dash for the big barn about a quarter mile in front of him? If they saw him in the open, he was done for. He decided instantly. He sprinted toward the barn, his soggy moccasins slipping in the wet grass. He uttered a silent prayer that he would have at least sixty seconds. If he was not seen in that length of time, he could reach the barn safely. If he could not outrun them in the hills and woods, and could find no suitable place to hide, he would take his chances on this building. But it would be an obvious place to look. He didn't care. He was desperate, and this was his last hope of refuge.

The weathered gray wooden structure loomed above him, and as he ran around to one side, he spied the half-open double doors and darted inside. He paused, leaning his hands on his knees, gasping, water dripping in puddles around him. After a few seconds Jay cautiously ventured a look outside toward the woods. He saw no one—only a few cattle with their backs to the blowing rain, heads bowed. Another crack of lightning made his chest constrict, and a clap of thunder shook the ground under him. He ducked back inside, his breathing beginning to come a little easier. His strong physical condition was an asset, as he began to recover quickly. He smelled the musty hay and the ammonia of urine as his eyes gradually grew accustomed to the gloom. The rain pounded on the roof, and water dribbled through in various places. The barn was a large one and looked to be many years old.

A thump and a sudden movement a few feet away sent him leaping back against a post. He looked for a weapon. Then the shuffling noise came again and he let out his breath in a rush of relief as he saw the head of a horse thrust over a stall door a few feet away.

He padded cautiously toward the far end of the barn, where the double doors stood wide open, forming a square of gray afternoon light in the black wall. He glanced at the stalls as he passed. Only one horse was in evidence.

When he peered out, the sight that greeted him brought another rush of fear. Three figures were walking slowly and spread-out down the slope from the woods. It was the sheriff and two of his men. They were moving cautiously but steadily, heads turning from side to side, hat brims bent down and streaming. One man held a rifle, while the sheriff and the third man carried only their drawn six-guns.

He felt panic. His decision to hide in this barn had been a mistake. Now he was trapped.

He darted silently toward the door he had entered at the opposite end. Perhaps he could slip out without being seen, keep the barn between himself and his dogged pursuers, and run toward the opposite side of the valley to the woods, or make it to one of the other outbuildings without being seen.

But as he reached the big wooden door and started to slip through, he caught sight of a figure striding, head down, toward the barn from the direction of the bunkhouse. He jumped back, then glanced quickly at the wooden ladder to the loft. No. That would be the first place they would look. The lone horse might be his salvation. Praying that the animal was not some half-broken mustang or some high-spirited, nervous racehorse, he slipped up to the stall, talking softly to the horse. He reached out slowly and

11

touched the velvety nose. The horse jerked back with an alarmed snort.

"I haven't got time to get acquainted," Jay muttered, and vaulted lightly over the stall door. The animal sidled away and whinnied softly, ears erect and eyes wide. Jay slid along the wall of rough wood and burrowed quickly into the deep straw piled in the back of the stall. He took care to be sure he was entirely covered, leaving only his eyes and the top of his head exposed. He held his breath and listened intently. For an agonizing minute or two, all he could hear was the pounding of his own heart and the raging of the storm outside. Thunder rolled in continuous crashes, and he could feel the wood next to his head reverberate. Lightning flashes reflected from the walls. He lay on his left side, eyes fixed on the top of the stall door, and wished he had secured some sort of weapon, like a club or a pitchfork. But he was empty-handed, and felt very vulnerable. If discovered, he would have no choice but to give up immediately and hope they didn't shoot him on sight. At the very least he would be taken back to jail in Washington Camp and chained up until his trial so there would be no chance of getting loose again. Sheriff Dawson was a humorless, surly type whose mood would not be improved by an exhausting chase through the hills in the heat and then the choking rain. Jay could expect some rough treatment from him as payment for his escape.

The first sound of voices startled him. They were indistinct but coming closer. The booming of the thunder and the drumming of the rain on the roof kept him from hearing any of the words. His eyes were fixed on the top of the stall door, but the horse kept shifting nervously, partially blocking his view. More muttering of conversation. Then he could make out the strident voice of Sheriff Dawson raised in anger.

". . . know he must be in here some . . ." A loud crack of thunder drowned the rest of the lawman's words.

"Ah'm very sorry, suh, but there's no one in this'ere barn," another voice said. "Ah just come up here to shovel out some o' these stalls."

Several figures moved into his line of sight and paused near his stall. Jay froze and held his breath. A black man wearing a soaked hat with a sagging brim leaned his elbow on the stall door. "I'd a'seen anybody was they to come in here in the last little bit."

"Two of my men are combing those woods up yonder," Sheriff Dawson continued. "But Mel, here, swears he saw him run across this field toward this barn. But it was raining so hard, he didn't see where he went. We been chasing this killer for the last hour. And we been hot on his tail since he busted out o' jail at Washington Camp. I'm Sheriff Dawson, and these men are my deputies."

"Yessir, but—"

"No 'buts' about it, man. We're searching this barn from top to bottom. If he's in here, we'll find him."

"Might be good was you to check with Mr. Clyde McPherson, the owner o' this here spread before—"

"We ain't checking with nobody, nigger! Outa the way. We got a killer to find."

The sheriff brushed past the black man, and Jay heard him giving terse orders to his two deputies, ordering one man to the loft and the other to start searching the stalls at the far end. "If you flush him out, give a holler. If he tries to fight or run, shoot him. I'm not . . ." His voice trailed off, and another crash of thunder swallowed up all sounds.

Would they search the only occupied stall? Jay was itching in a dozen different places from the wet clothes and the tickling of the straw. Somehow he had to get out of here. A mortal fear came over him, a fear that this sheriff had no intention of taking him back, that he was mad clear through and only looking for an excuse to shoot him as soon as he was spotted. Jay knew he had the speed to outrun these men, but he couldn't outrun a bullet. He had

13

made a fatal mistake by leaving the cover of the wooded hills to seek refuge here.

Just as he was pulling up his legs to crawl out and try to make a break for it, the black man reappeared, and Jay froze again. The man unlatched the stall door, swung it open, and stepped inside, a bucket in hand. Jay watched the man's legs under the horse's belly. He poured some oats into the wooden trough on the opposite side of the stall. "There ya go, big fella," the man crooned to the horse, stroking his neck. "Have a good feed, now."

He turned to go out. As he swung the door shut behind him, a blaze of lightning lit up the stall, and the man's glance rested for an instant on the straw pile in back. Their eyes locked. Jay saw the black man's eyes widen and his mouth open an instant before the wavering lightning flash flamed out. Jay sprang to a crouch.

The man glanced quickly around him and then stepped back into the stall, dropping the bucket he carried. "Stay! Stay!" he hissed quietly, waving Jay back.

When Jay hesitated, the man squatted and whispered urgently, "Mister, whoever you are, keep your head down!"

Then he straightened and pretended to start currying the horse. The realization hit Jay that this man was actually protecting him. He quickly wormed his way back under the pile of manure-fouled straw. He tried to steady his breathing as he listened to the stall doors banging while the two lawmen searched for him.

"You might as well come out and save some time!" Sheriff Dawson shouted, sounding very frustrated. "You haven't got a chance. You'll never get out of this barn alive if you try to escape!"

Jay shivered at the sound of this. He heard the lawman scuffing about in the next stall, kicking at the straw.

Jay had buried himself completely this time, so he could see nothing. But he knew when Dawson arrived at his stall. Flies were buzzing around the manure near his head, settling on the straw.

"Get that horse outa here, nigger," the voice snarled. "I need to look in here."

"I've already looked in here, suh," came the subservient tone.

"Oh yeah? Well, I'm lookin', anyway."

The horse squealed suddenly, and Jay felt the thudding of hooves as the animal backed up, nearly mashing his hand.

Dawson yelled as the horse whinnied shrilly.

"Whatsa matter with that damned thing?" Dawson was yelling.

"Down, boy! Easy!" The man's voice was soothing as the horse shied sideways and jarred into the wall. Jay cringed back and tried to shield his head from the hooves. He was afraid he would be uncovered, if he wasn't stepped on first.

"This hoss is a mite skittish yet, suh. He ain't been broke long. He knows me 'cause I takes care of him, but he don't take kindly to strangers."

"Animal nearly stomped me!"

Jay heard the stall door bang shut and the thudding of boots receding on the dirt floor.

Jay twisted his head and saw the man's legs as he followed the lawman outside and closed the stall door. Jay let out a long breath of relief, but he didn't move. He waited what seemed like a very long time. Once, he thought he heard voices, but he wasn't sure, since the thunder was still rumbling and grumbling as the storm moved away. Then for a time he heard only the normal sounds of the horse munching grain, swishing his tail at the flies that infested the place, and the dripping of water from the eaves.

Finally he decided he was safe. The lawmen must have gone. He crawled cautiously out of the straw and stood up.

"Come on outa there, mister." The black man's voice was steady behind the twin barrels of the shotgun he held.

# CHAPTER 3

JAY'S stomach churned as he slowly came forward, around the horse and out the door, as the man backed away, holding his weapon steady. Out of the frying pan and into the fire, Jay thought. Probably thinks there's a reward for me.

"Are you a murderer, like they said?"

Jay shook his head. He was too discouraged to trust his own voice. He had gone from despair to hope and back to despair. He thought he might have found a friend in this stranger. He might have known better. Most people he had met didn't help total strangers for no reason—especially if there was reason to believe that person was a criminal.

"March on down there to the bunkhouse," the black man ordered.

Jay walked ahead of him, his muscles stiffening up and aching with every step, the clammy clothes itching and clinging to him.

"Hold it there."

Jay stopped and leaned on the second rail of the corral fence, putting his head on his arms. He was tired, sore, and thirsty.

"They sure did want you bad," his captor said, coming

around to face him. "Just keep your hands on that rail while I see if you're armed."

He reached cautiously forward and patted Jay down while the young man stood, dejectedly, not moving.

"You part Indian?" the man asked, glancing at the high Apache moccasins and Jay's bronzed skin and dark hair.

"No." He was feeling so bad, the word came out just above a whisper.

"Why don't you talk to me, boy? You hurt or sumpin'?"

Jay took a deep breath and straightened his back, looking into the dark face of his captor, and the twin barrels of the shotgun.

"I'm okay."

"Tell me what happened?" The man's voice sounded a little less harsh, if not friendly.

Jay relayed the story of the wrestling match, and the footrace. Then he told of the town celebration, the fight with the nephew of the sheriff, his accusation for the accidental killing, and his jailing. "Been in jail there five days, awaiting trial," he concluded.

"You escaped?"

He nodded.

"You run 'em a merry chase through the woods, huh?" There was the hint of a twinkle in the black man's eyes.

Again Jay nodded.

"They shore had their tongues hangin' out." The man broke into a grin and lowered the shotgun. "That Sheriff Dawson deserves to lose one now and again. If he's the best they can do for a lawman down to Washington Camp, Duquesne, and Lochiel, they's hurtin'. 'Sides, I ain't let no man call me a nigger since I come out here and took to workin' for wages like a real free man years ago."

He looked Jay up and down. "Tell me sumpin', did you do it? Did you shoot that boy? Are you a killer?"

Jay shrugged. "No. At least I don't think my bullet could have done it. I've gone over it a hundred times in

17

my mind while I was in that cell, and I don't see any way it could have been me. Even by some sheer accident or a ricochet.''

"But they were bound to pin it on you anyway." The man bobbed his head knowingly. "I seen their type before. Oh, yes, I seen 'em plenty back home. What you gonna do now?''

"I don't know. Right now I need to get as far away from here as I can, as fast as I can.''

The sun burst out of the broken clouds that were hurrying off to the east in pursuit of the rapidly vanishing storm.

"You need to get outa them wet clothes.''

"I don't mean to put you out," Jay said. "But I sure could use a drink of water, too.''

"No bother. The spout's over there. Then I've got some extra clothes you can use. You're a mite taller than I am, but at least you'll be dry.''

A stream bisected the narrow valley. Jay followed the man's lead to where a long rusty pipe led out of a rocked-up pool and filled a mossy wooden stock tank with clear cold water. He thrust his head under the pipe and drank, forcing himself to stop before he felt too full.

"My name's Walker Hyde," the black man said, thrusting out his hand. Hyde was dressed more like a cowboy than a laborer, wearing worn Levi's, a cotton shirt with rolled-up sleeves, a bandanna around his neck, and a brown felt hat shoved back on his head. Even with the high-heeled boots, he stood only about five feet seven. His grip was strong, and Jay noted the corded muscles in his forearm. He looked sinewy-tough and could have passed for a man of forty, with his smooth, mahogany face, even though Jay guessed he was probably at least a decade older than that.

"Jay McGraw. Pleased to meet you—and many thanks for saving my life in that barn. I believe that sheriff and his boys would have killed me on the spot if they'd found

18

me. I owe you my life. What can I do to start repaying that debt?''

"You ain't in my debt, just as I ain't in no man's debt. You can thank me by gettin' a good night's sleep while those clothes o' yours are dryin', and then headin' out and not lettin' that sheriff ever catch up to you again.''

"By the way, what'd you do to that horse?'' Jay asked. "If he hadn't spooked like that, Dawson would've found me for sure.''

Hyde grinned. "Don't rightly know. That stallion couldn't have seen no filly. Maybe it was that hoof pick I slapped him with.''

His laughter was contagious, and Jay joined him, whooping at the thought of the red-faced sheriff being crowded against the side of the stall by the big horse. Not until he laughed did he realize how tense he had been. He felt better for it, and seemed to have established a rapport with this black cowboy.

"C'mon down to the bunkhouse and I'll get you some clothes.''

"Did the sheriff and his boys leave?'' Jay swept his gaze around the ranch.

"Shore did. Reckon they thought you wasn't here after all. They looked around at the bunkhouse and the main house. Even poked into the privy. They was pretty disgusted.'' He chuckled. "They figured you must be hidin' in the woods somewhere around, 'cause they didn't actually see you come down here.''

"Who's the owner of this spread?'' Jay asked.

"Clyde McPherson. He's a good man.''

"Is he in the house?'' The place looked deserted. "He might not take to the idea of harboring a fugitive.''

"No. His daughter's home, but he's over at Fort Huachuca with all three of his boys. They drove a couple dozen horses over there to sell to the Army. I expect they'll be back tomorrow. Mr. Mac trusts me to take care of things,''

Hyde said with a trace of pride. "The old Mexican cook, Felipe Fernandez, is at the house too."

"You the foreman of this place?"

"Naw. This here's just a little greasy sack outfit. Mr. Mac pretty much ramrods things himself. There's just Mr. Mac and me and the cook and three hands—two Mexicans and one white man."

Jay was still surprised that the owner would leave his daughter in the care of two older men in a place so wild and remote. This was Apache country. There was no law in this part of the territory except at the various mining towns and, of course, some troops at Fort Huachuca, a few miles away to the east.

They went into the bunkhouse, which was a log structure, similar to the house but much smaller. The one room contained one door, four wooden bunks, two windows with glass, a small table, and four chairs, one of which was broken. Leather chaps and two rain slickers hung on wall pegs. A potbelly stove squatted in the center of the room, its black chimney pipe projecting through the roof. Two harp lamps hung from the ceiling.

Walker Hyde rummaged in a large bag at the foot of his bunk. "Here, try these." He tossed Jay a flannel shirt and a pair of faded Levi's. "Reckon you'll have to make do with those moccasins. Don't have no spare shoes or boots that'd fit you."

Jay gratefully stripped off his clothes and pulled on the dry ones. The Levi's were too short but otherwise seemed to fit. The high moccasins would make up for the length. He tugged off his wet footgear. The smooth wooden floor felt good under his white wrinkled feet. He would go barefoot until his moccasins were dry, his bruises were healed, and his feet had regained their normal appearance.

"You can stretch out on my bunk and sleep for a while before supper, if you like."

"Why are you doing this for me? You're not thinkin' to

20

turn me in for a reward, are you? Because there isn't one," Jay said defensively.

Jay detected a hurt look in the man's dark eyes. His face went solemn. "I ain't about to turn you in to nobody. Least of all, that Sheriff Dawson. I know what it is to be hunted. I run off from a Mississippi plantation once back in the fifties. You say you're not a killer, and I believe you. I'm a pretty good judge of men. You're young, and you don't have the face of no killer. I could be wrong, but I don't think so. You stretch out there and sleep. You look tuckered out. I'll get these clothes dry. After a good supper, you can slide outa here, easy like, if you've still a mind to run. I can point you toward Harshaw or any one of the towns in the Huachuca Mountains. Did you know the Apache name means Thunder Mountains?" He grinned and left the room, swinging the door shut behind him.

Jay swung his legs up onto the blanketed bunk and groaned as he lay back. He was so tired! He was hardly aware of the scratches and bruises. The afternoon breeze swept through the open window near his head, soothing him to sleep within minutes.

# CHAPTER 4

IT was late afternoon when Jay awoke. He felt rested, but he had stiffened up considerably. It was a familiar stiffness that had come after many football matches and wrestling bouts back home. But it was a good soreness that he could work out quickly enough, he realized, as he swung his bare feet to the plank floor. He twisted his torso back and forth and stretched his arms. No pulled muscles, no strains. Only the bottoms of his feet felt bruised and tender from pounding across the rocky hillsides in the soft moccasins.

He stood up and walked to the window. The heat that had blanketed the area before the storm had not returned. He inhaled deeply of the freshness of the damp grass and earth. He was glad for this solitude, glad that all the men were gone from this bunkhouse. He was in no mood to be fending off questions.

He was thirsty again, and hunger pains were beginning to gnaw at his stomach.

Where to from here? He had no money, no gun, no horse, not even a hat, and he was being hunted by a sheriff's posse. He needed to get out of here tonight, he decided. No telling when Sheriff Dawson might return after he and his men failed to find him in the woods. Dawson didn't strike him as the type who would just give up and go home. They would probably commandeer some horses and keep on combing the hills for him for at least another day or so. They knew he was on foot and couldn't go far unless he stole a horse.

He sighed and turned away from the window. But then, this was the kind of challenge he had welcomed most of his life. And up to this time the challenges had come mostly from athletics. His pursuit of excellence had honed his natural abilities and built up his speed, agility, and power. But most of all, athletics had strengthened his mental discipline.

He sat down on the edge of the bunk just as the plank door opened and Walker Hyde came in.

"You about ready for a little grub, Mr. Jay?"

He grinned. "I could sure use something."

He followed Hyde outside and around the corral toward the main house. But Hyde stopped at a large, tree-shaded wooden table about thirty yards from the house and threw his leg over a bench.

"We'll eat out here. Lots cooler than inside. This here's a small outfit, like I said. Mostly we eat in the house with Mr. Mac at least three times a week if the weather's not good enough to eat outside. It's mostly like family here. Mr. Mac don't hire nobody he can't treat like one of his own kin. If he do hire somebody he ain't sure of, they eat out here until he is sure."

Jay nodded, marveling to himself at the trusting nature of this Mr. McPherson. A man so trusting of strangers and employees could well find himself shot and robbed by some saddle tramp posing as an out-of-work cowboy.

The Mexican cook appeared from the back door of the log house. He brought a steaming iron pot of beans and set it on the table, and a tin plate of soft tortillas beside it. He followed that up with a pot of coffee and a tiny bowl of honey. That was it. The Mexican cook, Felipe Fernandez, returned to the house without a word. Nor did Walker offer to introduce him.

"Does he speak English?" Jay inquired as he filled a tortilla with hot beans and folded it over.

"Some. Felipe is a good man, but keeps to himself mostly. Just does his job and minds his own business. But he's been here longer than anybody and is very faithful to Mr. Mac. I seen some of my people like that with masters in Mississippi before the war. It was almost like they was workin' for wages."

"This is good," Jay said, around a mouthful of food. "No vegetables?"

"No garden truck this year," the black man agreed, filling two tin cups with coffee from a pot Fernandez had placed on the table. "Been awful busy this year. Never got around to plantin' nothin' in the spring. Felipe didn't put himself out none this evenin', since Mr. Mac and the boys are gone."

"This Mr. McPherson just raises horses to sell to the Army?"

"Raises a few. Catches more, though. Wild ones. Has to break 'em to saddle mounts before the Army'll take 'em. They'd rather have bigger, better-bred remounts, but they sometimes have to take what they can get. We have to take the rough edge off the mustangs. That's where I come in. Been doin' this kinda work for about a dozen years now. To tell you the truth, I've about come to the end o' my string. Been broke up a good deal over the years. I'm gettin' a little old to be bustin' wild broncs. Don't rightly know what I'll do when I have to give it up. And that time ain't far off. I think Mr. Mac is lookin' for a good bronc buster now."

Jay stirred a spoonful of honey into his black coffee. "You just keep a few longhorns for your own use, then?"

"Oh, no. They's usually a lot more grazin' in this little

24

valley. But this land's not fenced. They's all scattered up into the hills hereabouts. Prob'ly a couple hundred head, give or take. Mr. Mac hires a few extra hands—mostly Mexican vaqueros—each year to round 'em up and brand 'em. Not just longhorns. A goodly number o' crossbreeds. Don't have too many miles to drive 'em to market, so they don't lose what fat they get from this good grass. Not like the Texas herds a few years back.''

"You've never had any trouble with rustlers or Apaches?''

"Only once that I recollect. Mr. Mac, he's a sly fox. Stays quiet and goes about his business. And he stays small. That's how he stays out of sight in this tiny valley. Like I said, this is a little greasy sack outfit. Nothin' much here to steal. No raiders bother with us back in these hills.''

Jay sipped his coffee and said nothing. But he wondered about what this man was telling him. He had heard tales, and seen evidence himself, of Apache raids on small isolated ranches such as this. Hitting small ranches, killing and burning and stealing all the stock, was one of their favorite tactics. And this place was conveniently on the way to Mexico, even though not on the direct route most of the raiding bands took when fleeing across the border to their hideouts in the Sierra Madre.

"What happened this one time you had trouble?''

"Oh, somebody run off a bunch o' the stock. Come in here one night last year when all of us was gone 'cepten Felipe. Cleaned out about fifty head o' cattle that was grazin' out here. All we had left was a few strays when we got up into the hills to round 'em up. Never did find out who done it. We suspicioned it was part of Old Man Clanton's gang, but we couldn't prove nothin'.''

Shadows lengthened as they ate, stretching toward the upper end of the gently sloping valley. The clear gurgling stream flowed from the wooded upper end, bisecting the long narrow grassy valley and disappearing into the wooded lower end. In addition to the wooden stock tank, part of the water had been diverted to fill a good-sized man-made pond.

Perhaps three-quarters of a mile away, at the lower end of the valley, a small herd of about fifteen horses grazed. They appeared to be hobbled.

"Did Mr. McPherson start this ranch?"

"Yessir. 'Bout eight year ago. Back when the Apaches were raisin' sand. Me, I only been here since '79—about two year. That sawed-plank barn was here when Mr. Mac came, though. Don't know who built it, but it's pretty old. Somebody had lived here before. Maybe the Indians run 'em off. Who knows?"

Jay nodded and swept his gaze around at the peaceful setting once more. The barn was the largest building on the spread. There was also the small bunkhouse, a large, peeled-pole corral off to one side, with a holding pen beside it, an outhouse below that, a couple of nondescript wood and tool sheds, and just behind him the solid, low-roofed log house situated just where the valley floor began its slope up toward the scattered trees.

"I need to get out of here tonight. No tellin' if that sheriff might be back."

He didn't much want to leave, but he knew he had to put some distance between himself and his pursuers. Thanks to this man, he had escaped them so far. On foot, he could travel by night and sleep by day until he was out of these hills. It probably wouldn't even be safe to stop in Harshaw or any of the small mining towns in the area. His best bet was to head for Tucson. But Tucson was many miles to the north and west, probably too far to travel on foot, especially across so much open country. Between the June desert heat, lack of water and a hat, and the threat of Apaches, there was a good chance he wouldn't make it.

He could possibly get to Tombstone and get a stage to Tucson. From the Old Adobe he could buy a ticket on the cars of the newly built Southern Pacific to California. But all this would take money. And all he had left were the clothes on his back. And at the moment, even they belonged to someone else.

"Sheriff Dawson won't be back here tonight. He's gone on for now." Hyde waved his hand in the general direction of the Mexican border and grinned. "I made sure. By the time they find out you ain't down south, or west of here, you'll be long gone."

Jay studied the look of mirth on the black face, puzzled as to why this stranger, who had no idea if he was really a criminal or not, would choose to help him.

"Why are you doing this for me?" he asked.

"You asked me that before. I've had some dealin's with that Dawson. He's a bad one. He thinks I'm just a dumb nigger. That's what I want him to think." He grinned and tapped a finger to his head. "I know what he's like, even if he does pretend to wear a badge and be a man of the law. And I'd rather believe you than him."

He grinned again and poured himself another cup of coffee. "I tell you what, if you gonna—"

"You're not my daddy!" a strident female voice interrupted them.

Jay jerked around on the bench in time to see a young woman in a riding skirt, checked shirt, and low-crowned hat stomp across the front porch of the house. Felipe came out behind her and said something with his back to them.

"I always take a ride this time of the evening, and this day isn't any different just because the men are gone!" she retorted, turning to jerk loose the reins of a saddled pinto that was tied to a porch support.

She pulled the pony's head around and swung expertly into the saddle. Without a backward glance she cantered

27

off, riding easily and gracefully as she rounded the big horse corral and headed toward the upper end of the valley.

Felipe muttered something in Spanish as he stood looking after her. He wore a disgusted look on his seamed face. He ran one hand through his thick shock of black hair, spat another Spanish expletive from under his heavy, graying mustache, and retreated into the house.

"Who was that?"

"Karen McPherson. Mr. Mac's daughter I told you about. She comes out here to spend the summers from a boardin' school back in Tennessee. They ain't doin' much for her, I don't expect, since she's gotten mighty sassy. Lots worse than last summer."

"Where's her mother?"

"Carried off in an Apache raid about six, seven year ago, they tell me. Ain't been seen or heard of since. She's either one o' the squaws o' some buck or she's dead," he stated matter-of-factly. Jay shuddered at the mental images this conjured up.

"Any other kids in the family?" Jay inquired.

"A son. Randolph. I've only seen him a couple times. He hangs around up to Santa Fe and Taos. Ain't no account. Took to drinkin' and carousin'. 'Bout broke his daddy's heart. He only comes down this far south when he can sober up enough to make the trip and wants to borrow money from his daddy. Say, why you so interested in this family, anyway? Just who are you? You ain't told me nothin' about yourself."

Jay shrugged. "Nothin' much to tell. Brought up in western Iowa. Eight brothers and sisters. I'm third oldest. My people migrated there from Illinois about forty years back when the area first got settled. Good farmland."

"You a farmer? I seen enough grubbin' in the earth to last me two lifetimes when I was owned by a Mississippi cotton man."

28

"No. My daddy is a brick mason and owns his own brickyard and kiln. Two of my younger brothers are goin' into the trade, but it wasn't for me. I worked enough to be able to go off to college in Des Moines. Thought I wanted to take up medicine, but I only lasted two years. Didn't make the grade and ran out of money about the same time," he added before Hyde could ask why. "I was pretty good at athletics, but that was about all." He shrugged. What he failed to say was that he missed playing professional baseball only because he was playing with a sprained ankle the day the scouts from Cincinnati came to watch him. He also failed to mention that he was the best his college had in football and wrestling and was the fastest sprinter in that part of Iowa.

"What happened?"

"I came home from school and tried to get a job in the little town of Vail where I lived. Couldn't settle down to a dull job workin' in a store or in my father's brickyard. I felt like the best part of my life was passing me by and I didn't know what I wanted to do with myself. Finally decided to see a little of the world. Didn't want to join the Army; I'd heard a lot of tales from the older men around town about what they went through fighting for the Union. I didn't want to get restricted by the military as bad as I felt restricted at home. Had to do something where I felt free and unrestrained, you know what I mean? Had to strike out and try different things. Maybe find out what I want to do with the rest of my life."

"So you come out here?"

"Yeh. Worked just long enough to get a stake. Said good-bye to my family and took the UP cars west from Omaha."

"How long you been in this part o' the country?"

"Just over a year. In the Arizona Territory the last nine months."

"I can generally judge a man pretty close. If you'd a

mind to shoot somebody, it wouldn'ta been no chile. If it was your bullet, it had to been an accident," Hyde pronounced with the finality of a judge. "They can't hold you for no accident."

"They did."

He gave Jay a searching look. "Where you goin' when you leave here?"

Jay had been pondering that very question, and didn't have a ready answer. Finally, when Jay was silent for a long minute or two, Hyde offered, "You're mighty welcome to spend the night here. Mr. Mac and the boys won't be back until sometime tomorrow."

Jay shook his head. "Thanks, but I have to go. You may have thrown them off my track for now, but I need to put some distance between me and them. You've done more than enough for me already. I don't want to get you in trouble if I'm discovered here."

Hyde waved him off. "I ain't worried about that."

"Where are my moccasins?"

"Felipe's dryin' 'em near the stove. I'll get 'em."

He disappeared into the back door of the house. He was back in a minute carrying the footgear draped over one arm. "They's mostly dry." He handed them over. "Those Apache moccasins?"

"Yes. I bought them from an Apache scout at Fort Bowie a few weeks back. They're made for desert travel."

"You run footraces in these?"

Jay nodded as he folded the buckskin back and thrust his hand inside to check the remaining dampness. "I smear some pine pitch on the soles. Helps my footing, but it's not as good as the running shoes I had back home."

"I'll get your clothes." The older man went to a rope line strung from the back of the house to a tree and returned with Jay's Levi's and shirt. The blood had been washed out of the knee and the mud and sweat from both garments, Jay noted. They had dried soft in the hot wind.

30

"Thanks for all your help." Jay stuck out his hand. "Maybe I can return the favor someday."

Walker Hyde gripped his hand. "You're mighty welcome, young man."

"I'll leave your clothes in the bunkhouse." Jay got up from the table and started away.

In a few minutes he was changed. As he stepped out the bunkhouse door he noted the sun was down behind the tree line at the lower end of the valley. The sky was still a pale blue with streaks of red and gold.

He had made up his mind to head for Tombstone. He needed money, food, a weapon, and a horse. All could be obtained in the boomtown in the San Pedro Valley. It was sufficiently distant from Washington Camp for now. He could blend in there among all the strangers coming and going in that fast-growing, wide-open silver town. Then, after he had made a small stake, he would move on to some safer place farther away where no one would look for him.

He hefted the small bundle tied up in a blue bandanna. Hyde had prepared him three soft tortillas wrapped around some of the still-warm beans. He had declined the offer of a canteen, since he planned to stick to the hills and could find enough small streams and hollows of rock to drink from.

He raised his hand in farewell to the black man, who still sat at the table near the house. Hyde didn't move.

Jay found a narrow spot in the stream, leaped across on some rocks, and headed off at a fast jog toward the wooded slope on the far side of the valley. With any luck he had another hour and a half before it would be too dark to see and he would have to stop and make camp. He slipped up through the sparse growth of small cedars that quickly changed into the denser growth. A few minutes later he slowed to a walk and looked back. The ranch and the valley itself had disappeared from view as if they had

31

never existed. Tombstone was northeast of here. Hyde had given him some rather vague directions. He would go as directly across country as the terrain would allow, guiding by the position of the sun and using whatever trails or roads he could find for easier travel. He would have cover and water from small streams by staying in the hills. But he would have felt safer with some kind of weapon.

It was about ten minutes later that he saw the Apaches.

# CHAPTER 5

HE was walking through some heavy stands of stunted cedar when he caught a movement out of the corner of his eye. He immediately froze. Moving only his eyes, he sought out whatever it was that had attracted his attention. His heart began to pound when he identified, through small breaks in the trees, several Indians on horseback. They were about forty yards away, downhill and slightly to the right of him, riding slowly in single file. He tried to count them as they moved in and out of his vision through the dense foliage. He would have dropped to the ground immediately, but they were angling toward him, and he feared a sudden movement might give him away. As near as he could tell, there were six or seven of them. He held his breath, hoping that the faded Levi's and the brown-and-yellow plaid shirt would blend in with the foliage around him.

As they came closer, down a trail on the opposite side of the wooded ravine, they dropped partially below his line of sight. But he could easily make out their long black hair and their headbands. They were painted for war. Two of them wore blue Army blouses with the sleeves cut off. One wore a loose, dirty-white shirt, and the rest had bare torsos, breechclouts, and high moccasins, turned down and tied. All of those he could see were riding white men's saddles, and two carried lever-action Winchesters. Scouts from nearby Fort Huachuca or Fort Bowie? He didn't think so. There was no white man with them. Their headbands were not the red flannel customarily worn to distinguish the scouts. And he had never seen scouts painted up like this. Probably Bronco Apaches—renegades on the prowl for whatever they could get.

In spite of the heat, a cold chill went over him when one of the riders turned his head and looked directly at him. The black eyes, above the yellow horizontal lines of paint on his cheekbones, seemed to bore into his hiding place. But apparently the greenery and the dimness of the twilight in the undergrowth were sufficient to screen off the view. The Indian swept his gaze in the other direction, and a few seconds later, the line of bobbing riders passed below his view on the trail into the bottom of the ravine.

Jay let out his breath in a long, silent sigh.

He waited a good five minutes before he moved, and then it was with the utmost caution. Being careful not to step on any dead twigs or dry leaves, he moved away to his right—opposite the way the riders had gone. He was all eyes and ears. About a hundred yards away he made a long sweeping curve and started north again, down into the dip at the head of the ravine. He angled up the other side, keeping to the thickest growth of juniper and oak that he could find. All the while he watched carefully downhill where the war party had disappeared. A few birds still chirped, but otherwise the wood was silent.

Suddenly he came out onto the narrow trail that the riders had been following. He stopped to examine the ground. There were some other hoofprints besides the marks of the unshod Indian ponies. This trail had seen frequent use. The deeper impressions of iron-shod hooves could be seen plainly, going in both directions. Some of these tracks were obviously older, some having been partially obliterated and washed out. One set of tracks in particular seemed to have been very recently made. Small clumps of fresh mud had been dug up by a fast-moving horse, and small stones had been kicked out of the ground that were still dry on the underside. Someone had passed here since today's rain.

He straightened up and looked around. He made no pretense at being a tracker, but he was curious as to who this rider was. Where did this trail lead? To a mining camp? He wished he had asked Hyde to draw him a map or give him more detailed directions about this area.

Every sense alert, he started up the trail at a fast walk. He glanced at the sky. The last of the dying sunlight had turned it into a pale bluish yellow, casting an almost artificial brightness over the hills.

Jay knew he was taking a big chance walking this trail. He could very well run into another group of Apaches just around the next bend. But this was much easier traveling, and he could put some distance between himself and the Indians before he had to stop and find a place to camp. He would just depend on his quick reflexes to warn him of any impending danger. Every few minutes he stopped and held his breath, listening for any unusual sounds. There were none. As he swung along at a fast walk, the thought suddenly occurred to him that this trail behind him might lead right to the valley he had just left, back to the McPherson ranch and the two older men who were by themselves.

The thought brought him to a standstill. He wiped his damp brow with a shirtsleeve. Should he go back and try to warn them? He was probably already too late. The riders would already be there by now. Maybe if they were under attack, he could help. But he had seen no guns, except the shotgun the black man had held on him. Not even in the bunkhouse had he seen a weapon. But then the hands would have taken their sidearms with them on the drive to Fort Huachuca. He wavered. Should he return? The Indians may have gone on down the trail past the valley and paid no attention to it. Yes. Chances are they had. No reason to think they would bother that small ranch. But he couldn't really convince himself of this. To an Apache, guns and horses were power and wealth. And there were horses at the ranch. And that war paint . . .

He had to go back. Even if he arrived only in time to bury them, he couldn't desert two men who had befriended him, fed him, and probably saved his life.

Just as he turned to run back down the trail, his ears caught the thudding of hoofbeats, fast approaching. The sound was coming from up the trail in the direction he had been headed.

He jumped off to one side into the woods. He could see about fifty yards up the trail before it bent out of sight.

The hoofbeats grew louder, and a horse and rider leaned into view around the curve. The figure on the pinto looked familiar—the checked shirt, the flat-crowned hat, the way the rider sat the saddle. It was the girl, Karen McPherson!

He dropped the bandanna of food he had been carrying and sprang out, waving.

"Ho! Hold up! Stop!"

Startled, she checked her horse briefly, but then kicked his flanks and plunged straight at him.

"No! No!" he yelled, waving his arms desperately. But she was not stopping for any stranger on this lonely trail, he realized as he threw himself to one side, rolling out of the way.

"Apaches!" he roared at her as she swept past him, leaning low over the animal's neck.

"Damn fool!" he muttered as she disappeared around the next bend.

He took off at a fast pace, running down the trail after her. He had no hope of catching up with her before she overtook the Indians, but he had to try to do something.

Just *what* was the question. He was unarmed. Maybe the Apaches had gone into camp by now and she would ride right past them before they saw her or could pursue. It was probably a vain hope. Thoughts of rape and torture sprang into his imagination. Before he realized it, he was sprinting on the downhill trail. His feet flew over the ground in long strides. He was nearing the bottom of the wooded ravine where the trail bent to the right out of his sight. He forced himself to slow down and stop before he reached this bend. He stepped off the trail into some cover and listened. Nothing. He could hear nothing but his own harsh breathing that sounded very loud in the stillness. Even the birds had gone to roost in the dusk.

He wiped the sweat from his face and allowed his breathing to steady down slightly. It wouldn't do to go charging into something unknown without the wind and strength to run or fight.

He started walking at a brisk pace, still catching his breath. Still no sound of horses or humans. Maybe the Indians had gone on past the valley and the girl was safely home by now. He fervently hoped so. And with every step, this hope grew stronger as he saw and heard nothing. Every sense was alert as he walked silently in his moccasins. But his eyes were less and less able to penetrate the gathering gloom.

A woman's scream split the quiet woods. And as quickly was cut off. His stomach tensed into knots at the sound. It was what he had been dreading to hear. He jogged forward silently in the fast-fading light. He judged the sound to have been maybe two or three hundred yards away. After about a hundred yards he slowed to a walk, moving forward like a cat, sensitive to any sight or sound. Perfect stillness.

He froze at the crack of a branch breaking, followed by the guttural sound of a human voice.

He crept forward, eyes straining to penetrate the darkness. Then he heard low voices again, maybe forty yards away. Staying in the middle of the trail to avoid any brush or leaves, he moved as noiselessly as a shadow until he guessed he was near where the scream had sounded. It was then that he spotted the wink of a campfire through the foliage downhill and slightly to his left. Near a creek, he guessed. It took all the courage he could muster, and about twenty minutes, to work his way close enough to see. And what he saw was what he had feared seeing. It was the camp of the Apaches. But where was Karen? Was the choked-off scream her dying scream? That she would be killed, he had no doubt, and she would be put through much worse before death, he imagined. And he had heard no shot. But if she had ridden upon them suddenly, they might have reacted and killed her without hesitation.

Belly-down, he scanned the campsite. He could see only five of the Indians. Where was the sixth? He was sure he had seen six of them earlier. Standing guard somewhere outside the circle of light? Maybe even now slipping up to put a knife between his ribs? The thought gave him a chill, but he fought down the panicky urge to look around behind him. He would be night-blind from staring at the campfire, anyway.

But where could the girl be? They hadn't hidden her in a wickiup, since this bunch had not even thrown up one or two of the brush shelters they commonly used.

Three of the men were passing around a crock jug of something. There was some discussion, some fast, harsh words between two of the men. One of them yanked the jug from the other's mouth, slopping some of the contents onto the ground. The other two were roasting what looked to be parts of some kind of rodent carcass over the flames on two sticks. Sweat glistened on their bare chests and backs as they moved around.

Jay scanned the camp carefully again. If the girl wasn't here, there was no reason for him to stay. But the next trick would be to get away without being seen or heard.

A quick movement caught his eye at the edge of the firelight. He saw her booted legs and the riding skirt. He leaned to his right to see around the tree trunk that had blocked his view. Yes, there she was, seated on the ground, her back to a small oak, her arms tied to either side of the trunk, hatless and disheveled dark hair falling across her face. He couldn't see her eyes, but apparently she was conscious, since her head was erect. She had been gagged with the headband of one of the warriors.

Thank God she was alive! Maybe they were saving her for when they had eaten and gotten drunker on whatever was in the jug. Maybe they were saving her to trade for something else they wanted even more. But, judging from the way two or three of the Apaches looked at her, gesturing and laughing, he didn't much think so. They would use her and kill her. Bronco Apaches in war paint. They were out for plunder. They were moving toward Mexico and would take no prisoners. He guessed they would cut a destructive path on their way. For all he knew, the McPherson ranch might be their next target. This girl had just fallen into their laps like a ripe plum.

He ground his teeth in frustration. He would give almost everything he owned, which wasn't much, to have a fully loaded Winchester in his hands at this moment.

One of the savages threw on more dead branches and the flames blazed and crackled. The jug was passed around some more and pieces of roasted varmint were ripped off, smoking, from the green sticks.

Suddenly, the sixth Apache appeared from the far side of the firelight, gliding in with a rifle in hand. He said something to the others and pointed back over his shoulder. Then he leaned his Winchester against a fallen log and reached for the jug. Apparently he had been out on some sort of scout.

Jay was in a dilemma. He was one man, unarmed, against six Apaches with guns and knives. Strong and quick and sober he was, but he was also no fool. Should he try to get away quietly and run for help from the ranch? He was not sure how far it was, or exactly which direction, since the sun was gone, and the trees blocked most of the sky. If or when he got to the ranch and brought back Hyde and Fernandez with guns, the girl could well be dead, her throat slit in some drunken orgy, or, worse yet, tortured to death with knives, burning sticks, and all the ingenuity of the Apache mind. He could always sacrifice his own life to save the girl by some wild attack that would set her free to run while he occupied all six of them long enough for her to get away. That was only a fleeting thought. Heroic as it sounded in his head, it would very likely only get both of them killed. And he wasn't ready to die yet, heroically or otherwise, if he could live and still get the job done.

He cast about for some other plan, but there seemed to be none. His initial alarm and instinctive fear of these painted savages had calmed during the long minutes he lay and watched them. He had faced long odds in athletics before. But the consequences of losing then were only pride, bruises, or broken bones. Here it was his life.

Maybe he could try backing off into the woods and howling like some strange ghost. Playing on their superstitions, especially while the Indians were drunk, might work. On the other hand, it might just put them on their guard, one or two of them watching the girl while the others investigated. Or it might scare them into killing her, breaking camp, and bolting.

No. Better to rely on their carelessness. The big fire, the loud talk, the dropped rifles, the lack of a guard all advertised that they expected no pursuit. He waited. He would let the liquor do its work. He hoped it was strong enough and the jug full enough to debilitate all six of them before they attacked the girl. He put his head down on his crossed arms and rested.

# CHAPTER 6

IN spite of the deadly danger hardly more than a hundred feet away from him, he dozed.

A loud exclamation from the camp must have roused him. He raised his head. The fire had died down, and no one had replenished it. Jay didn't know how long he had been asleep, but he was instantly alert. Two of the Indians were sprawled out on their backs, passed out. The other four were apparently in an argument. One of them started toward the girl. In one swift movement, he caught the front of her checked shirt and ripped it open. The biggest—and evidently the drunkest—of the four grabbed his arm and jerked him back from the captive. The vociferous wrangling in Apache began again. It was apparent they were arguing over who was to have her first. Even the four who were still on their feet looked pretty much the worse for the liquor.

The horses, minus Karen's pinto, were picketed at the edge of the firelight in the woods. Jay had seen them moving around when he first came up on the campsite. He had not come in downwind of them since there was no wind, but they were on the opposite side of the small clearing.

He had to move. It was now or never. He had lain still

for so long he was stiff. He rose carefully to his hands and knees, then to his feet. Being very careful where he stepped, he moved away until he was out of earshot of the camp. Then, running as quickly and quietly as he could, he made a wide circle around the camp, going down to the edge of the small creek and almost stepping off into it in the dark. He turned his ankle on the creek bank as it was, and had to grit his teeth against the pain of it for a few seconds. He tested the ankle. It wasn't sprained. He crept back up toward the camp. Careful, careful, he told himself as he tested each step before he put his full weight down on each foot. The argument seemed on the verge of exploding into violence. Good. That might give him a chance. But a slim one.

Their fire was flickering low, but the low light caught the glint of a knife blade as one of the Apaches moved toward the others.

Jay eased closer behind the tree where the girl was tied. A dry branch snapped under his foot. He froze. But they were too drunk and making too much noise to pay any attention to small noises.

He crept up behind the small oak where the girl was ·tied. Her captors were nearly shouting at each other.

"Stay quiet, Karen," he whispered hoarsely with his head on the shaded side of the tree. She didn't move. "Karen!" he whispered urgently. "I'll get these ropes off your arms. Be ready to run!" She still gave no indication that she heard him. Jay had his mouth nearly at her ear. She had to have heard him.

One of the Apaches lunged at another with his knife, and two bodies locked together, rolling on the ground. But both of the other Apaches had the same idea at the same time.

They went for the girl.

One of them reached quickly around the tree and slashed

her leather-strap bonds. Jay leaned back and held his breath as the knife arm came within a foot of him.

They dragged her to her feet. The two drunken warriors were still rolling around on the ground behind them, neither able to secure an advantage or to make a final, deadly thrust. Of the two Apaches who had grabbed the girl, one seemed almost sober. He was the larger of the two, and he was clearly asserting his authority and prior rights to the girl. He was a muscular man with an almost flat nose and a straight gash for a mouth. The eyes, in the last light of the low-flickering fire, were black beads. The smaller, drunker of the two was arguing in harsh guttural tones, but he made no move toward his bigger companion, who still held the knife he had used to cut her bonds. The girl was still gagged with one of the headbands, but her hands and feet were free. She did not struggle as the Apache gripped her. With one last explosive utterance at his companion, he began dragging her off toward the other side of the clearing. He avoided the still-struggling bodies on the ground, and half dragged, half carried her by the waist into the darkness on the other side of the horses at the edge of the clearing.

Jay moved back quietly but as quickly as he dared and circled around toward the girl. The horses were sidling and jerking nervously as the two warriors, locked in mortal combat, rolled under their feet. Jay took a quick longing look at the Winchester leaning against the log near the dying fire, but there was no chance of his reaching it without being seen.

He jerked up short as the crashing of brush told him the location of the Indian and Karen in the darkness. They were about twenty yards from the clearing. He listened. The crashing stopped, followed quickly by the sound of tearing cloth and a low grunting.

Jay moved in on the sound. He squatted and felt quickly around him for some kind of weapon. Nothing but dry

43

leaves and grass. He swept his hands in a wider circle. He felt a branch. But as his hand closed on it, he knew it was rotten. Then he felt a rock. About the size and shape of both his fists. He hefted it. Perfect weight.

He bounded forward and threw himself at the two figures he could not see. He slammed into the side of a sweaty, naked torso and both of them went down. Jay swung the rock where he guessed the man's head to be. But the Indian's arm was upraised, and Jay's wrist glanced off, nearly dislodging the rock from his fist. Jay gripped both his arms around the man's waist as the Apache brought down his fist on the back of Jay's neck. Jay was vaguely conscious of the girl scuttling away from beneath the flailing bodies. Jay reached for the man's knife in the scabbard at his waist, but his knife and breechclout were gone. The Indian was naked. On sudden impulse, before the Indian could completely react, Jay brought his knee up into the man's groin as hard as he could. A gasp and a groan escaped the mouth by Jay's ear. The Apache relaxed momentarily. Jay swung the rock. It connected with the Indian's head with a dull thump, mashing one of Jay's fingers under it in the process. An agony of pain shot through Jay's finger, and for a second or two he was unaware that the heavy body had slumped to the ground at his feet.

He dropped the rock and grabbed his hand. "Karen! Karen!" he cried. No answer. Was she still gagged? He staggered this way and that, his arms outstretched in the darkness, feeling for her. Then he found her. She was sitting on the ground a few feet away. He yanked her to her feet just as some alarmed Apache voices came from the clearing. He saw two forms, outlined in the dim firelight, coming toward them.

He scooped the girl under the arms and propelled her toward the horses, hoping the Apaches coming from the firelight had temporary night blindness. The girl seemed limber and unresponsive. If only she could run on her own!

He let her slump as he reached the nearest horse. He tried to jerk the rein loose from the picket line. It was fastened securely. Damn! For want of a knife, he might still be killed. No time to find a sharp rock to saw it through. In desperation, he lunged at the picket line, which was strung between two stout trees. The taut line gave but did not break. He fumbled with the knot that held the nearest horse to the picket line. It took all his discipline to be calm for a few seconds and concentrate on the knot. The leather lines were tied but had not pulled up into a tight knot as a rope might have. He dug his fingernails in, wedging the leather straps apart.

A grunt warned him at the last second of the knife thrust coming from his left. He spun and the knife grazed the belly of the horse behind him. The animal gave a startled squeal and jumped sideways, bumping the horse beside him. Jay aimed a kick at the figure, regretting that he wasn't wearing boots. The knife went flying. Anger surged through him, driving out all remaining fear. He waded into his assailant, fists swinging. A hard blow to the chest and then a left smashed into the Indian's nose knocked him backwards.

He whirled to the knot again. Suddenly the knot was loose and Jay reached for the girl with one arm as he held the horse with the other hand.

"Up! Get up! Let's go!" he shouted. He almost threw her up onto the animal's back, then sprang up behind her. Before he could get full control of the horse's head, the animal bolted straight ahead through the campsite, leaping the dead log and the fire. Jay caught a glimpse of three prone figures on the ground as his mount crashed into the darkness on the other side. He struggled to keep his seat on the bare back and hold the girl in front of him as the spooked horse plunged blindly ahead.

"Hold on to the mane!" he yelled into her ear, reaching around her waist to hold her. He was subconsciously aware of the bare flesh he was touching. Bending low to avoid the branches whipping past, he struggled to turn the horse toward the trail to his right. He dimly remembered where the trail was, and it seemed it was downhill to his right. The horse had no bit. Whether they had removed it for grazing, or were just using the headstall and one leather rein as a hackamore, he didn't know, but only his superb balance and leg strength kept him astride the animal as it leaped and crashed through the woods.

He had not been able to break the picket line and set the other horses loose, so he had to assume the Apaches would be after them quickly. But he had seen three bodies stretched on the ground. Two of them he knew were passed out from drink. The third may have been dead or wounded by a knife thrust. Of the remaining three, one he had hit with a rock. That left two able to pursue. But did they have the heart or will for it? He had to doubt it. But he couldn't rule it out. He had stolen both the girl and one of their horses. These braves had been painted for war. Unless they were just too drunk to care, how could they let this affront go unavenged?

Jay had been pulling the rein against the horse's neck, and suddenly the animal responded with such a sudden move to the right that Jay was nearly unseated. He had to grab wildly for the girl and the horse's mane at the same time. Even so, it was several seconds before he got his balance again. And when he did, he realized they were on the trail heading toward the creek at the bottom of the ravine. The hooves were drumming on the soft earth, carrying them in the general direction of the McPherson ranch.

# CHAPTER 7

"**I** understand you're the young man who saved my daughter's life," Clyde McPherson said to Jay in the main room of the log ranch house the next afternoon.

Jay nodded but did not speak. The older man looked at him thoughtfully. Clyde McPherson was a tall, stately man with graying brown hair. He had a sweeping mustache, a straight nose, and clear gray eyes. He wore dusty boots, jeans, and a leather vest over a white shirt. He and his men had just ridden in from Fort Huachuca, and he looked very tired.

The rancher was silent for what seemed like several minutes before he spoke again. Jay was feeling very uncomfortable.

"You, of course, have my undying gratitude," he finally went on. "I don't know if you are aware of the fact that my wife was taken by the Apaches several years ago. She's never been found. I don't know if she's dead or alive. I hope to God she's dead," he added, a slight choking in his voice.

"Walker Hyde told me," Jay said.

"Karen's asleep in the back bedroom just now," the rancher went on. "She seems to be in a state of shock and was not coherent when I got home. Walker told me what happened, but I'd like to hear the details from you."

Jay related briefly the incidents of the night before. Now and then, during the story, McPherson interrupted him with a question.

". . . so we were able to ride back here and rouse up Walker and the cook. But there was no pursuit," Jay concluded. He shrugged. "I guess they'd either had enough or didn't know how many men might be at this ranch and didn't want to risk a night attack. And I believe at least one of them had been killed or badly wounded by one of the others. They were painted up for war. They may have just broken camp and gone on down the trail toward Mexico or wherever they were headed when we ran into them."

"Hmmm. You have a lot of courage. You might have kept on going. You could have easily gotten yourself killed. In fact, I can't think of any white men who have come off a winner in an encounter with six Apache warriors."

Jay reddened slightly, shifting his weight on the home-made wooden couch. "They were all drunk and fighting among themselves, so I had complete surprise on my side."

"Even so . . . even so . . ." McPherson reached for a box of cigars on a side table, flipped open the lid, and offered him a selection. Jay declined with a wave of his hand.

"It still took someone with a good head on his shoulders as well as courage to do what you did and pull it off successfully."

"I was very lucky."

"Luck is an essential part of life. None of us would get very far without a good dose of it now and again."

McPherson selected one of his slim cigars, bit off the tip, and spat it to one side. He took a match from a small

48

brass cup on the table, struck it on a boot heel, and puffed his smoke to life before speaking again.

"Young man—Jay is it?" he said, recalling the brief introduction from Hyde. "You could just about name your price. Whatever I have, within reason, is yours. Because my possessions would mean nothing to me if my daughter had been killed or carried off into captivity. I don't think I could have survived another loved one being taken by the savages."

"Mr. McPherson, I really don't want anything from you."

"Surely there's something. Do you need money? A job? You need a horse?"

Jay hesitated. Apparently Walker Hyde had not told his employer the whole story. Should he trust this man and tell him that he was on the run from the law at Washington Camp? Surely the rancher wouldn't turn him in. Not after what had transpired. He glanced at the big Colt the rancher wore. If he confided in this man and guessed wrong, he would not be able to force his way out and escape. He decided quickly to go with his instinct—and his instinct told him to confide in Clyde McPherson.

"Sir, there's something you need to know," Jay began, and went on to give him the whole story, leaving out nothing.

The rancher, who had sprawled sideways in an easy chair across from Jay, heard him through to the finish, puffing slowly on his cigar and not changing expression.

"I judge a man by what he does, not by what someone else says he does," McPherson said when he had finished. "Even if your bullet did kill that kid, it was strictly an accident. And they'd have a helluva time proving you did it, anyway, unless they find the slug."

"I do need a job," Jay said. "When I escaped, I didn't think it the appropriate time to ask Sheriff Dawson for my money, my horse, or my gun."

A grin split the rancher's face under the wide mustache. Then he became serious again. "That presents a problem. I'd give you a job in a minute, but we're mighty close to Washington Camp, and I wouldn't want Dawson walking in on you someday when you're not expecting it. I've known Dawson for a spell. You couldn't have done anything that would've gotten him more riled than breaking out of his jail. You probably would have been better off staying and taking your chances with the judge."

Jay shook his head. "I don't think so. That whole town was in an ugly mood toward me after I won those races and those bets. Then, after I beat Tige wrestling, Tige's girl kinda took a fancy to me. Even if some judge had let me off, I don't think I'd have gotten out of town with my hide intact."

McPherson waved his hand. "Well, all that's past history. I know you can ride. Can you rope?"

"Never had much practice at it," Jay admitted.

"No matter. There are a hundred things need doing around here. If you want to stay on here awhile and work for me until you get a stake, I'll hire you and pay you a decent wage. You may not be safe from the law here, but I'm willing to worry about Dawson if or when he shows up, if you're willing."

Jay grinned and gripped the rancher's outstretched hand. "You bet."

"You'll need a pair of boots," McPherson said, glancing at the high moccasins Jay wore.

"Oh, I can work in these."

"Not in the job I have in mind for you."

"What's that?"

"Breaking wild horses to the saddle."

"I'll sure give it a try. I've broken a few before, but I don't know how they'd compare with some of these wild mustangs you have here."

"Well, I know you're an athlete and must have good

50

coordination and balance and strength. I figure you can handle it. There's an element of danger, of course, as you know. You could get busted up some. Hyde has managed to last several years doing it, but he's an exceptionally tough and durable little man.''

"I won't be taking his place, will I? I don't want to take a man's livelihood, or his pride. He's been awful good to me."

"No. I'll have enough work for the both of you come two or three days from now. In the morning my men will be riding out west of here to take delivery of a herd of a dozen or two wild ones that some vaqueros are rounding up for me down along the border. Good pickin's down there since the Apaches started raidin' back and forth again. Not many cowboys want to risk trapping wild mustangs down that way. But these vaqueros I hired would ride into hell itself if they thought they could make a few silver pesos doing it. Anyway, rest up a day or two, and you'll have all the work you can handle for a while."

Jay got up, thinking how tired he still felt. He rubbed a hand across the stubble on his face.

"You can clean up and shave in the bunkhouse. There's an extra bunk there, since one of my hands chose to stay at the fort and join up. Fighting Apaches sounded more exciting, I guess, so I paid him off. Anyway, Walker can get you a razor. Fernandez should have supper ready about six."

Jay put his hand on the door latch as the rancher got to his feet and dropped his cigar butt in a nearby cuspidor.

"Oh, hold on a minute."

Jay paused.

"I have something for you."

The rancher disappeared into the next room. In a minute he was back, carrying a package wrapped in rawhide.

"I bought this for Karen when she was here two summers ago, but she didn't want it, so I just put it away."

He unrolled the rawhide to reveal a holstered revolver. "I wish she had had it last night. It might have helped. Go on. Take it," he added as Jay hesitated.

Jay slid the gun out of the tooled Mexican holster. It was a nickel-plated Colt Lightning with a four-inch barrel and pearl grips. The bird's-head grip fit his hand perfectly.

"You said you had a Lightning, so that's what gave me the idea. It's been fired a few times, but it's just like new."

Jay flipped open the loading gate and turned the cylinder to be sure the weapon wasn't loaded. It was a beautiful weapon—a .38 caliber, he noted.

"Hope it's not too fancy for you. Figured Karen might be inclined to carry it if it was lighter and looked nice. But, for some reason, she doesn't think it necessary to go armed out here."

"I appreciate the offer, Mr. McPherson, but I can't take this."

"Why not? You need a gun, don't you? I'm not going to leave you unarmed while you're working for me. No telling when Dawson or one of his deputies might show up. I just wish you'd had it last night. It might have evened up the odds some. Besides, some men don't favor the bird's-head grip on these. I guess the heavier-caliber single-action Colt or Smith and Wesson is more popular. These 1877-model double-actions are favored by store-keepers, drummers, gamblers, Wells Fargo expressmen, and the like who don't want to carry a big heavy sidearm but still want something a little more accurate and far-reaching than a derringer. I've fired it a few times, and it throws a slug out there with pretty good accuracy. Doesn't carry the charge of a .44, but in most instances, it'll get the job done for you."

"You don't have to sell me on the Lightning," Jay said. "All those are the reasons I bought one in Omaha before I came out here."

"Some men I know consider it a lady's gun, but I don't."

Jay grinned. "Don't worry about that. I don't care what anybody else thinks. I tend to think and do for myself."

"I'll just bet you do."

The loops on the cartridge belt were full. Jay belted the weapon on. McPherson handed him the rawhide wrapping that still contained two boxes of cartridges. "Here. That piece won't do you much good without these."

"Thanks."

"Just consider it a small token of my appreciation for what you did last night."

"I sure hope your daughter's all right."

The rancher's face became serious. "Physically, she's fine. But time will tell about her emotional state."

Jay moved toward the door again.

"Oh, by the way, what size shoe do you wear?"

"About a nine."

"I've got some old boots of mine that are nine and a half that might fit you. I'll send Walker down with them after I've had a chance to look for them. If you feel up to it, why don't you plan on riding out with my other two men in the morning to collect that herd. Might be good to get away from here for a few days, just in case Dawson and his deputies are still looking for you. Besides, I'm one man short since Jack decided to join the cavalry."

# CHAPTER 8

JAY and the two McPherson wranglers went into camp the next evening while the sun was still two hours above the western horizon. They had not made contact with the Mexican vaqueros or the mustang herd as expected, but their own mounts were showing definite signs of fatigue.

Walker Hyde, former wrangler and bronc buster, had stayed behind. Jay got the feeling that the genial black man had put many a hard mile behind him, and it was beginning to tell on him. Jay got the impression that he was still a strong, faithful employee, but, due to his years and injuries, he had been relegated to the role of general handyman.

The two men Jay rode with were good enough trail companions and seemed competent enough. Eddie Flynn was a whip-thin Texan of about twenty-five with hooded eyelids that made him appear to be half asleep all the time. Carlos Guaderrama was an Arizona-born cowboy in his early twenties, who, according to his own declaration, had been astraddle a horse almost since he could walk. In spite of his name and the fact that he was bilingual, he spoke with only the slightest trace of a Hispanic accent. He had a smooth, round face, black hair and eyes, and displayed a wisdom beyond his years.

Both men seemed to accept Jay at face value—a young drifter in need of a job whom the boss had seen fit to hire to replace a departed hand. They asked him no questions about his past or his background, but seemed talkative enough when the conversation concerned the ranch or the job at hand. Eddie and Carlos had heard the story of his dramatic rescue of Karen McPherson, and it seemed to Jay that they treated him with unusual respect, if not with awe. He caught them, now and then, studying him when he wasn't watching, as if to discern what type of man this was they were being told to work with. They had no idea how scared he had been at the time.

Jay pulled the California-style saddle off the long-legged sorrel he had selected for himself and turned the hobbled animal out to roll or graze. While Guaderrama collected some dead brush and sticks for a fire, Flynn rolled himself a smoke.

They were about thirty-five to forty miles southwest of the ranch and well down out of the Patagonia hills, near the border.

"I don't like this area," Carlos said, breaking a dry limb over his knee into a usable size. "This is Apache country. They've been crossing the border along here for many years. There are no ranches in this area."

"I saw a log ranch house not ten miles back," Jay said.

Carlos nodded. "But did you notice it was abandoned? John Foster, his wife and son and two hands were killed there three years ago. The Apaches tried to burn it down, but a rainstorm put out the fire. No one has lived there since."

The three men broke out some slab bacon, a frying pan, and a small sack of cornmeal to prepare a meager supper. Jay took the three canteens to the nearby steam to refill them. The ride had been long and dusty. They were camped at the base of a small hill where Sonoita Creek meandered toward the Santa Cruz River in the distance. The stream was bordered by several gnarled old cottonwoods and hemmed in by willows. Beyond the stream to the west and south stretched a broad grassy valley that ran for several miles in a northwest-southeast direction, spanning the border of Mexico. As Jay squatted by the sluggish stream, he could look up under the trees and make out, in the distant blue haze, the bulking mountains of northern Sonora.

He finished filling the canteens and capped them. Then he stood up. He took a last look south. His eyes were caught by smoke rising—a lot of it. Was a grass fire burning itself out across the valley? He looked again, slitting his eyes in an attempt to focus better on the distant veil. That wasn't smoke, he suddenly realized. That was grayish-tan dust. Try as he might, he couldn't make out what was raising such a cloud. There was no wind to speak of—hadn't been all day. It was unlikely that it was some distant dust devil being whipped up across that vast open space in front of him, and it didn't have the shape of a dusty whirlwind—there was too much of it, drifting slowly up and away. It was the type of dust raised by a large trail herd.

He came back to the campfire and mentioned what he had seen.

Carlos's head jerked up from the coffeepot he was setting on the fire to boil. "What? A herd, you say?"

"I don't know. Couldn't see what was raising all that dust. Looked too big and too far away to be our horses."

Carlos went to his saddlebags on the ground nearby and took out the field glasses he had borrowed from Clyde McPherson. He disappeared at a run up the long hill behind the camp until he was above the level of the trees bordering the stream. In a few minutes he was back.

"That's a cattle herd, all right. And heading this way, right up the valley."

"Who'd be driving cattle up out of Mexico through

56

here?'' Eddie asked, squatting on his haunches and squinting through the smoke of his cigarette.

"No one who values his hide *or* his herd," Carlos replied with a puzzled look on his face. "This is the easiest route, but no Mexicans or Americans have been trading across this area for a long time because of the danger of Apaches and rustlers and Mexican banditos. They must be many and well armed to try such a thing."

"Looks like a big herd from the size o' that dust cloud."

Carlos nodded and put the coffeepot back on the fire. They went ahead with a leisurely supper. Jay still felt distinctly hungry when he finished his meager ration of bacon, fried cornmeal cake, and coffee, but he said nothing.

However, Eddie Flynn spoke up. "Damned if I don't wish I had a good juicy rabbit to go with this," he groused, leaning back against his saddle and picking his teeth with a piece of dry grass.

"Where're we supposed to pick up that herd o' mustangs?" Jay asked. He had ridden all day with the two wranglers, letting them lead the way and not asking any questions. He was the newcomer here.

"Right along the eastern side of this valley," Guaderrama replied. "Since we just struck the valley about three miles back, we could meet up with them most anywhere along here, even on down to the line."

To Jay, this seemed a little haphazard, but maybe that was the way of things in this part of the country. Vague timing and the most general of directions.

They washed up the frying pan in the nearby creek, and Jay slipped off the borrowed boots and stretched out on the grass to watch the gaudy, glorious sunset. Eddie and Carlos lounged nearby, Carlos lying on his side with his head propped up on one hand. Eddie lay on his back against his saddle with his fingers laced behind his head, his hooded eyes slitted nearly shut.

The slow-moving herd was probably bedding down for

the night well south of them, they decided, so they paid no more attention to it.

The setting sun blazed up in a long, gradually changing, silent show of color in the pale-blue sky and then began to fade slowly into a lingering twilight. The broad sweep of deserted valley before them looked peaceful. Jay felt himself relaxing and beginning to doze. The unneeded cooking fire died to embers in the stillness.

"Reckon that was part of Victorio's Warm Springs Apaches that grabbed the McPherson gal the other night?" Eddie said, to break the long silence. "He and a bunch of his followers took off from San Carlos Reservation a while back."

Jay had no idea what kind of Apaches they were, but Carlos answered, "I doubt it. Victorio's band has more discipline, from what I've heard. They wouldn't have gotten falling-down drunk and started fighting over a girl." He glanced at Jay for confirmation. "Isn't that what happened?"

"They were plenty drunk, all right." Jay nodded. "Whatever was in that jug was my biggest ally."

"Prob'ly tiswin," Eddie Flynn said.

"Tiswin?" Jay queried.

"Yeah. They make and drink the stuff on the reservations. It's against regulations, but the soldiers generally look the other way, if it doesn't make 'em too wild. And the civilian Indian agents won't call in the military unless they're forced to."

"You ever seen or tasted any of it?" Guaderrama asked.

"Seen some. Never tasted it."

"A cousin of mine over at Fort Apache saw some made and stole about a quart of it. We tried it one night. Whew! It's bad."

"What's it made of?" Jay asked.

"As I recall, he said they put a sack of corn in the creek to soak until it begins to sprout. Then they put it in one of their big willow ollas with plenty of water and keep it as warm as they can. Then, when it's sprouted and soft, the squaws mash it up good with wooden clubs to release all the juices. Then they set it in the sun to ferment. Takes about three weeks before it's ready. When it's ready to drink, it looks like sour buttermilk and smells like a sewer."

"You actually drank it?"

"Sure did. My cousin and I and another fella. Tasted like a mixture of dead fish and rancid milk. But one drink of it would make a jackrabbit slap a wildcat." Carlos grinned.

"Maybe so, but I don't see how one big jug of the stuff would be potent enough to put away about four out of six grown Apaches. Especially if they were used to the stuff," Jay said.

"If it was in a crock jug, it was probably some whiskey they stole from some white man," Eddie said. "They can't handle that whiskey. Injuns go outa their heads with that stuff."

"Well, whoever they were, I was lucky," Jay concluded.

"Renegades, probably," Carlos said. "With no leader. Jumped the reservation, stole some horses, out to raise some hell, do a little killing, and get drunk."

The desultory talk drifted on to other subjects until dusk had blackened into night and overhead the stars looked like diamond chips scattered on black velvet.

"I'll take first watch," Flynn volunteered, sliding the Winchester carbine out of the saddle boot as he rose.

No one objected, and soon Carlos and Jay were stretched out on their blankets. Jay was weary from a long, unaccustomed day in the saddle. That and the heat and the strenuous last few days put him to sleep quickly. His last thought was a quiet prayer of thanks that he was miles from Sheriff Dawson.

*     *     *

Jay didn't know how long he had been asleep when he was awakened by the sound of voices. Probably Eddie waking Carlos for the second watch, he thought as he rolled over and sought a more comfortable position on the blanket and the grass.

"Jay!"

At the urgent sound of his name, his eyes flew open and he sat up.

"They're pushin' that herd right up the valley," he heard Flynn say.

Jay rubbed his gritty eyes and stood up. He smelled dust on the night air. The moon, newly risen, revealed a herd of several hundred cattle less than a half mile away. In the dim light he could see them moving like a massive, shaggy carpet. There was a low rumbling, and the air was charged with their presence. He could hear an occasional bawling, and now and then a shout from one of the point riders hazing a stray back into line.

"They should be bedded down for the night by now," he heard Guaderrama say.

"Unless they started late in the day," Flynn said.

"Strange," Carlos said.

"Why's that?" Jay asked.

Carlos hesitated before replying. "I have a feeling about this herd. No one drives herds back and forth across the border here anymore. No one but Apache raiders or rustlers drive cattle across here anymore."

"Don't mean nothin'," Flynn said. "Could be some rancher a ways north of here has got himself a good price on a bunch o' beeves in northern Sonora. These drovers are just pushin' them up the valley at night cause they got good moonlight and can avoid all that damned heat in the daytime."

The herd was flowing past them now, the animals fairly docile.

60

"Keep 'em bunched up and movin'!" one of the outriders yelled at another as he passed closer to them in the dark. "We don't want'em smellin' that water and makin' a stampede for it until we get to the river."

His voice sounded so close in the night air that Jay felt a sudden chill of apprehension.

The three stood still, watching and listening, and gradually the herd passed them, heading north.

"That rider's voice you heard a few minutes ago," Carlos said as the sounds of the herd faded, "was the voice of Billy Clanton, one of Old Man Clanton's sons. And that Clanton bunch and the ones they hang around with have never been known to do an honest day's work. You can bet if they're driving those cattle, they've been stolen from the Mexicans."

"I thought Old Man Clanton left these parts," Eddie Flynn said as they prepared to bed down again.

"He moved over to the Animas Valley in southern New Mexico last year," Guaderrama replied. "But he left his ranch near Tombstone to his boys, Ike and Billy. Nobody knows for sure, but everybody says it was Old Man Clanton and the outlaws who ride for him that massacred those thirty-three Mexicans driving a pack train of smuggled goods up through Skeleton Canyon a while back. Killed all of them except one boy, and he's hiding out for fear of his life as the only witness. Those Clantons are a bad lot—a real bad lot. And that gang that rides for them—Johnny Ringo, Charlie Green, Billy Lang, Tall Bell, Curly Bill Brocius, Jim Hughes, Tom and Frank McLowery—leeches, the lot of them. They live on the work of honest men."

"How do they get away with it?" Jay asked, stretching out on his blanket as Carlos took the rifle to stand guard.

"Fear. They're mean. Just as soon kill a man as swat a fly. Nobody's come up with any hard evidence against them. They're careful to leave no witnesses. Even if they did, I think most people would be afraid to testify. They

61

prey a lot on the Mexicans across the border, and Arizona authorities have no jurisdiction down there.''

"I hear tell there's a feud shaping up in Tombstone between the Earp brothers and Sheriff Behan," Flynn said. "The Earps are claiming that Sheriff Behan is protecting the Clantons. Last time I was in town, things looked to be workin' up to a head.''

Carlos hefted the carbine. "We'd better get some sleep. We've got some hard ridin' ahead of us tomorrow. Jay, I'll wake you in about two hours to take the last watch.''

# CHAPTER 9

"HE looks like a mean one. Think you can handle him?" Carlos Guaderrama asked as he and Jay perched on the top rail of the six-foot-high corral.

"I'm sure gonna give it a try," Jay answered under his breath as he eyed the mustang that was charging around the enclosure. Walker Hyde and Eddie Flynn were sliding the chute gate shut on the far side. He glanced toward the larger corral, where the rest of the fifteen wild mustangs were milling nervously, awaiting their turn.

It was three days later, and the Mexican vaqueros who had gathered up this herd and helped Eddie, Carlos, and Jay drive them back to the McPherson ranch had been paid off and gone their way. Much to the relief of Jay. He had never seen such a cutthroat-looking foursome as those vaqueros. From the time they first made contact with the Mexicans, the day after the cattle herd passed their camp, Jay had not turned his back on them, and he had slept with his hand on his loaded Colt.

"I had the same feeling about them," Carlos confided after they had gone. "But the boss didn't hire them because they were charming and upright. He hired them because they could catch mustangs and they agreed to do it for twenty dollars a head in silver pesos or gold."

Jay shifted his weight on the rail and sized up his first adversary, conscious that he would be under close scrutiny as he attempted to break his first mustang. He estimated the animal to be about thirteen hands high—no more. And maybe eight hundred pounds. Eight hundred pounds of muscle, and mean, he thought. He fervently wished he had never let McPherson think he had any experience breaking horses. He had broken exactly one horse back home. Even though it had been larger, it was not nearly as fractious as this one. The only really wild mustang he had tried to ride since coming west had been a mount that some soldiers at Fort Bowie had given him as a practical joke. He had promptly been thrown. But this time he knew what was coming and would be ready.

No sense delaying this any longer, he decided, and reluctantly slid down off the rail into the corral, a coiled lariat in one gloved hand. He was glad the girl was nowhere in sight to see him make a fool of himself.

He shook out a loop and slowly approached the horse, which was nervously pawing and prancing on the far side of the circular enclosure. The mustang eyed him warily as he approached. Then, with a snort, he plunged away, circling the corral. Jay patiently stalked him, angling to head him off. Then he swung the loop and threw. A clean miss as the mustang galloped past. He felt foolish as he retrieved the rope and started again. He was vaguely aware that Walker Hyde had slipped into the ring to help. On the third try, his loop settled over the mustang's neck, and Jay dug in his heels to hold the rearing animal. At the same time he flipped the end of the rope to Hyde who gave it several turns around the snubbing post in the center of the corral and made it fast. After several jerks on the taut twenty-foot line, the mustang learned the choking effect of the slipnot and stood quietly, ears erect and feet braced. Jay took a bridle and walked up the line, talking quietly. But the horse was having none of it. He jerked and twisted.

64

But Jay, after letting him see and smell the bridle, finally managed to slip it over his head and fasten it in place.

Then, with Hyde's help, Jay got a rope around the animal's front legs and hobbled them. Following this, Jay held the horse by the bridle and threw on a saddle blanket. It finally stayed in place long enough for him to swing the forty-pound saddle up and on with one hand. Moving with speed and agility to avoid the kicking hooves, he darted in and managed to secure the cinch straps. He hooked the stirrup over the saddle horn to get it out of the way, and the mustang bucked and jumped as he tugged the cinch tight.

"Make sure she's snug," Hyde called from behind him. "I busted a collarbone one time when my saddle slipped on the first jump."

When the rig was in place, Jay retreated to the snubbing post in the center of the dusty arena and let the animal hop on his hobbled forefeet and get used to the weight of the saddle on his back.

"Whew!" he wiped a sleeve across his sweating brow. "I feel like I've done a day's work already."

"Just wait till you climb up on him—you'll *think* a day's work." Walker Hyde grinned. Then his face went serious. "You be careful, Jay. Ain't no bronc worth gettin' hurt for. Don't you fool around none with him. When he starts sunfishin', you quirt him good. The quicker he learns you're the boss, the better."

Jay approached the horse again. With one quick motion he reached down and yanked the slipknot loose and freed the horse's forelegs from the hobbles. He kicked them to one side and then got a firm grip on the dangling reins just below the bit as Hyde came up to loose the lariat from the horse's neck. When the rope was loose, the animal sensed freedom and jerked and jumped, half dragging Jay around the dusty corral. Finally, he stopped to blow, and tongued the bit in his mouth as he eyed Jay malevolently.

65

"Okay, fella, it's you and me," Jay said quietly. "Let's get this over with."

He hand-walked up the reins, and with no sudden moves, looped the rein around the neck. The animal trembled but did not move. Jay, holding the reins in his left hand, put his right on the saddle horn. He sensed the horse would try to jump sideways away from him as soon as he felt Jay's weight in the stirrup. He used the tactic Hyde had told him about when they had discussed this procedure step-by-step the day before. With his left hand he grabbed the mustang's left ear and gave it a hard twist. While the animal was distracted with the sudden pain, Jay swung himself aboard.

Just as his weight settled into place, the mustang threw his head down and his rear end high in the air. Even though Jay was expecting it, the violence of it snapped his body forward. Before he could recover, the horse threw up his head and smacked Jay in the face. A stabbing pain shot through his nose. Tears blurred his sight as he felt the warm blood flow. He fought to get his balance. His right boot finally found the stirrup. And just in time. The mustang began to twist sideways with every jump in an effort to throw off this thing on its back. Without both stirrups to brace against this force, Jay knew he would never be able to keep his seat. The mustang bucked and twisted and even reached back with his head to try to bite Jay's leg. Every time he threw his head back, Jay quirted him hard between the ears with the weighted butt of a leather quirt held to his right wrist by a leather thong.

Jay knew he had him now. With the grace and balance of an athlete, he kept his seat and rode the tiring animal to a standstill. The mustang gave one last effort with several mighty jumps, landing stiff-legged on all four feet, jarring every bone in Jay's body. Then, its resistance broken, the mustang gave a few halfhearted bucks and came to a stop, his sides heaving and his head down.

In the sudden silence, applause burst from Eddie Flynn, Carlos Guaderrama, and Walker Hyde, who had been watching the performance.

Hyde came up and took the animal's bridle while Jay climbed off.

"Mr. Jay, you look worse than you did after you tangled with those Apaches." The black man's face creased in a toothy grin.

Jay felt gingerly of his nose. It wasn't broken, but it would be swollen and tender for a day or two. He felt good about his first try. He could feel his confidence returning.

Flynn and Guaderrama were unsaddling the mustang and leading him away. A sliding gate divided a chute that connected this corral with the adjacent holding pen. As Jay wiped the blood from his face with a bandanna, he watched the wranglers slide open the gate and haze another wild mustang through the chute and into the corral. A bigger, dun-colored horse burst through into the corral and trotted around.

"You watch this one," Hyde said. "I seen him earlier. This jughead's liable to try to roll on you. Be ready to kick out and get shed of him if he does."

Jay nodded, eyeing this fresh animal, who bucked and stormed around the ring, challenging anyone to get near him.

"When you get this'n pretty well worn down, shake this slicker around his ears. Get 'im used to sudden motion. He won't spook later on."

Jay nodded and wiped the sweat from his face again as he glanced at the sun. He knew it was not yet ten o'clock in the morning. At this pace, it was going to be a long day. And I thought football was tough, he thought. Incredibly, Hyde had been doing this for years.

Apparently, the older man was reading his face. "You handle this one and I'll take the next one," Hyde said.

"It's a deal." Jay looked up toward the ranch house. Then he looked again. Karen McPherson was sitting in a rocking chair on the front porch. He threw up his hand and waved at her. But she gave no sign of recognition. And yet his heart gave a leap at the sight of her. He turned back to his work with fresh energy and determination. Even though she had not spoken, nor even returned his wave, he had the oddest feeling that he was her champion in the lists at some medieval jousting tournament.

By late afternoon he had broken four horses and Hyde had broken three. And both of them were ready to knock off and turn to some less strenuous chore. Even though he knew he would be sore in every muscle in the morning, he felt good about his day's work. He felt, without being told, that he had proven himself. And even though he had been thrown twice and had his left leg banged against the rail fence, he knew he had earned the respect of Hyde and the other two wranglers after the first ride.

He went to the bunkhouse that night weary but happy. The call for supper came shortly thereafter, and he, Hyde, Flynn, and Guaderrama were served at the outside table by Felipe Fernandez. Clyde McPherson and Karen were nowhere to be seen. He presumed they were eating indoors in the ranch house. Even though the owner had not been seen all day, Jay had the feeling that the ranch owner knew of the way he had performed this day. Jay's respect had grown tremendously for men who did this kind of work most working days of their lives. They must be toughened to it, and wise to all the tricks, he decided.

"Does the Army actually buy horses like this for the cavalry?" Jay asked around a mouthful of beans and bread.

"Yup," Eddie Flynn answered.

"Seems as if they could get better mounts than these."

"Sometimes they can; sometimes they can't," Carlos said. "The forts out here are a long way from good remount stock back east. And shipping is expensive. A few of the ranchers raise stock for the Army, but it's a chancy business. Predators, disease, and Indians all take their toll. Weather, too. If the Army can't get enough of the bigger, better-bred horses, they'll take these mustangs. They're generally a little smaller, but they're tough and used to feeding on grass, and they're a little narrower in the withers, so the McClellan saddles fit better. All of which makes for a good mount on a long campaign.''

"The Army don't issue none o' these mustangs to their Indian scouts. Some o' the scouts never have horses. But they can run for miles on foot without gettin' tired.''

"Army just gives 'em the regular soldier's pay of thirteen dollars a month," Hyde added.

"The mustang—he is an odd collection," Carlos said. "*Mesteno*—that was the original name—means 'stray.' They are wild range horses that are a mixture of cavalry thoroughbred remounts, eastern-bred workhorses, and wild ones that escaped and have been running free and breeding since the Spaniards came. You're liable to find all sizes and colors.''

"But to capture them—that takes some skill," Flynn said. "And what you were doing today—that's what it takes. You have to break 'em quick and hard or they're not worth a damn for anything. At least not for anything useful.''

"Is Mr. McPherson planning to sell this bunch to the Army too?" Jay asked.

"More than likely," Flynn answered. "Might keep one or two o' the better ones for the ranch here.''

The men finished off the hearty supper with a dessert of molasses on cornbread, washed down with some superb coffee from the culinary artistry of Fernandez.

"Fernandez does something to that Arbuckles that makes the best cup of coffee between Dodge City and San Francisco," Carlos remarked, leaving the impression that he had traveled to both places at some time or another.

Eddie Flynn rolled and lighted himself a cigarette, then leaned back, his hooded eyelids giving him a drowsy, satisfied look. "Feel like a game of checkers?" he asked Carlos.

"Not tonight. But I will take you on in some five-card draw."

"Same stakes as before?"

"Fine."

"You boys want to sit in? We could make it four-handed."

Jay and Walker Hyde both declined. It was too nice an evening to go inside the bunkhouse, Jay decided. And he was much too tired to concentrate on anything just now.

"Is Karen McPherson all right?" Jay asked after the two had left the table.

"I reckon so. Why?" Hyde replied.

"I haven't seen her outside but once since I brought her in here that night. She had most of her clothes ripped off and was in a state of shock. She never spoke a word from the time I tried to get her attention when she was tied to that tree until you and I and Fernandez gave her some brandy and put her to bed."

Hyde nodded. "That little missy's had the shock of her life, I expect. Did that Apache rape her?"

Jay shook his head, remembering. "Don't hardly think he had time. I jumped him too quick. But it was dark," he conceded. "Hard to tell for sure. Only the girl could tell us that. That's why I was asking if she was all right. I've never known a person to stay in shock for several days without saying a word."

"I have. I seen cases of it during the war. I expect you're too young to remember that."

Jay nodded. "I was only seven years old when it ended. But I've seen veterans who were made crazy by the war. There're a couple of them in my hometown. One of them became a drunk, and the other has been taken care of by his sister ever since he came out of the military hospital. He's just like a little child."

"Well, if we don't hear sumpin' of her soon, I'll ask Mr. Mac how she is," Hyde said. "He's pretty touchy 'bout his own kin. And I don't take no liberties 'bout pryin'. He's takin' care of her, and I reckon if he wants us to know how she is, he'll tell us. After all, you're the one who saved her."

"I saw her sitting on the porch today, just staring." Jay sighed and swung his leg around so he was astraddle the bench. He slipped the Colt out of its holster and laid it on the table.

"That's a mighty fine piece," Hyde remarked.

"Sure is. Mr. McPherson is a generous man."

"Ain't nothin' better than you deserve after what you done. Had me a nice Navy Colt once, but I traded it for whiskey. Been regrettin' it ever since. That old Remington I got now's in pretty rough shape, but I got it cheap. Shoots okay, but it ain't nothin' to brag on." He reached over and picked up the nickel-plated Colt Lightning. He turned it over in his hands, rubbing callused fingers over the pearl grips. Then he glanced up. "You know sumpin'? I'm tired of callin' you Mr. Jay. I think I'll call you Lightning from now on."

"Lightning?"

"Yessir. You're carrying a Colt Lightning, you first showed up here out of a lightning storm, and you're about the fastest white boy I ever seen. From now on, I'm callin' you Lightnin'."

"Okay by me. Lightning it is. But what about you? Don't you have a nickname? I haven't heard you called anything but Walker or Hyde." Jay grinned at him.

"My people were slaves since before my granddaddy," the black man replied seriously. "Walker was my uncle's name. I was named for him. My family name is Hyde. I don't know how we got it. But I'm proud of it and I plan

71

to keep it. No nickname for me." He got up from the table. "I got sumpin' to show you." He headed for the bunkhouse.

In a few minutes he was back, carrying something wrapped in a flat package of sheepskin. He carefully unfolded it on the table. Hyde picked up a folded paper and handed it to Jay. Jay spread it out. It was some sort of legal document, about eight by fourteen inches, printed on light blue paper. At the top, under a circular seal with a spread eagle, was printed STATE OF LOUISIANA. Beneath that, in ornate print, "Know all men by these presents, that I . . ." and most of the remainder of the document was handwritten in ink. Jay read on, looking carefully at the bold script.

> . . . Joseph Bruin of New Orleans, for and in consideration of the sum of thirty-two hundred dollars to me paid by Milton Wilson of Concordia Parish, La., the receipt whereof I hereby acknowledge, do bargain, sell, convey, transfer, and deliver unto the said Milton Wilson two negroes named and priced as follows, Ephram Foster aged about twenty-three years of age and priced at $1,600, and Walker Hyde aged about thirty years of age and priced at $1,600. Said negroes are both sold under a full guarantee against all the vices and maladies as prescribed by the laws of Louisiana, and I likewise warrant them sound and healthy and slaves for life.

The remainder of the bill of sale was printed, with names inserted in the blanks.

> To have and to hold the above-named slaves unto the said Milton Wilson, his heirs, executors, administrators, and assigns, to his and their proper use and benefit forever. And I, the said Joseph Bruin, do bind myself, my heirs, executors, or administrators, to protect and defend said property from all claim or claims whatever.

Dated at New-Orleans, the 18th day of March, Eighteen Hundred and Fifty-Nine

Signed: Joseph Bruin

Witnessed by
J. Hendley Simpson
John B. Smith

Jay read the document through again, slowly, letting the import of it sink in. Then he folded the bill of sale and put it back in its wrapping. The older man had shared a very personal part of his life with him.

"My owner give me that when he turned us all loose at the end of the war. Some o' my people stayed on to work for wages, 'cause they didn't know no other life. But I had to get out and go my own way. It was hard, though." He shook his head at the memory. "Couldn't read. Didn't know white folks' ways. Got took advantage of a good deal. Fact is, I found that some whites was meaner to each other than they was to blacks. Hell—" he grinned, "—ain't nobody gonna pay sixteen hundred dollars for a slave and then mistreat him to where he can't work. I reckon that's why I was treated better when I was a slave. Anyways, I brought this paper with me and took care of it until I could find a white man that would teach me to read. I wanted to read for myself what was wrote on there. That way I won't never forget where I come from. Well, anyways, I wanted you to see it."

"Thank you." Jay handed back the wrapped document. He didn't know what else to say. This man had not known what it was to be free until he was about thirty-six years old. Jay wondered how he himself would have handled that. Could he have made his own way as an illiterate in an indifferent, even hostile world as this man had? He doubted it. But then, a man never knew what he could really do until he was put to the test of necessity. He had found that out in athletics. He felt humbly grateful to have come from a good background. From now on, when he started to gripe about the small hardships of life, he knew he would think of Walker Hyde, freed slave and bronc buster.

# CHAPTER 10

THAT night, tired as he was, Jay slept fitfully. The soreness and the bruises were bad enough, but his swollen nose made breathing difficult. He tossed and turned, trying to get comfortable enough to doze off. He knew it was late when exhaustion finally took him.

When he woke, he was lying on his back, breathing through an open mouth. With a groan, he rolled over and tried to work some saliva back into his dry mouth. It was still dark outside. Faintly, he heard the thudding of hooves. The sound grew gradually louder. It sounded like two horses, and they were coming fast.

Jay, wide-awake now, padded barefoot across the floor and looked out the open window. In the pale light of a waning moon he could make out two riders as they pulled up in front of the ranch house and dismounted, tying their horses to the hitching rail. Their spurs jingled as they bounded up the stairs. Jay listened for their knock on the door, but it didn't come. Instead, he could hear the low murmur of voices on the still night air. A third person was on the porch, but the deep shadow cast by the roof hid his identity. Who were these men who came on fast horses in the middle of the night? Was something wrong? Were they bringing bad news? Jay assumed that the third party on the porch was Clyde McPherson. But he must have been expecting them if he was already outside, waiting. Or maybe he had heard them ride up and stepped silently out the front door. Jay's curiosity was piqued. What kind of business does a man conduct in the dead of night? Was this some emergency or something that couldn't be done in the daylight? He made a mental note to ask Hyde the next morning.

But, as the shadowy figures continued to talk, Jay could feel himself getting sleepy. He had to get some rest, or he'd be dead tomorrow, he thought. One of the men on the porch struck a match to light a smoke, but he turned away from Jay in the brief flare of light. Nobody I know, anyway, Jay thought as he turned back from the window and sought his bunk. With some little difficulty he dozed off and was sound asleep and dreaming when the cook banged the iron triangle to rouse all hands for breakfast just before sunrise.

When Jay forced himself up and started to dress, he felt as if he had been run over by a herd of stampeding longhorns. He thought he had been sore at times in the past, but every muscle in his body felt as if it had been bruised or strained. And the whole mass of pounded and stretched flesh had badly stiffened up while he slept by the open window and the cool night air. But not for the world would he have let on that anything was wrong as he pulled on his jeans and reached for his boots. His pride was on the line. Walker Hyde was certainly not showing any ill effects from the day before, and he had taken nearly the same pounding. The man was a wonder.

Soon after breakfast, Jay took Hyde aside as Eddie and Carlos headed for the bunkhouse. He told the black man what he had seen during the night.

"Don't rightly know who that mighta been, Lightnin'," Hyde said, shaking his head solemnly. "But then, I was tired, and I generally sleep like a rock, anyway."

76

Jay let the matter drop and turned to face another grueling day. At least it beat sitting in jail and waiting to be tried for killing a child. It was the most comforting thing he could think of as he pulled his borrowed hat down firmly on his head and glanced at the corral of wild mustangs that awaited him in the slanting rays of the early sun.

Surprisingly, once Jay had worked out his stiffness, he felt good. By suppertime, he and Hyde had finished breaking the remainder of the fifteen head, and he was ravenously hungry. And tonight it was fresh beefsteaks and beans and tortillas. Felipe Fernandez had to be the best cook west of the Mississippi, Jay decided. Either that, or he was unusually hungry.

They ate outdoors, as usual. As Jay was leaving the table, feeling pleasantly stuffed, he walked past the edge of the long front porch of the ranch house. And there, sitting in a rocker and warming herself by the slanting rays of the westering sun, sat Karen McPherson. She had her eyes closed and appeared to be dozing. He started to walk on, but then stopped and went over to the edge of the porch. It was the first time he had really seen her up close in the daylight. She had delicate features, but her face looked strong, with a firm chin and good bone structure under the fine-textured skin. Her pale face was framed by dark brown hair. All in all, a very attractive young woman.

"Karen?" he said. "Karen!"

At the sound of her name, her eyes fluttered open. The hazel eyes had a vacant look for a second or two, as if she were coming back from far away. Then she focused on him. But she said nothing.

"Karen, are you feeling all right?"

She stared at him with no sign of recognition.

"Don't you remember me? I'm Jay McGraw. I got you away from those Apaches."

She continued to stare at him, or rather, through him,

with no expression whatever. Jay got the eerie feeling she did not even see him. Had she somehow been blinded? But she didn't even answer.

"Karen?" He was disconcerted. He glanced around to see if anyone was observing him. The other men had gone off toward the corral, talking and smoking. He turned back to the girl, but she was now staring off toward the dull glow of the setting sun as if in a trance. Jay sighed and turned away. She apparently did not know him, did not even see him. He glanced back at the house. No sign of her father or the cook. What were they doing to take care of her? Was she like this all the time? Jay thought he might never know the real Karen McPherson. She could stay like that for years, just like the war veteran in his home town. Clyde McPherson might have lost his daughter just as surely as if the Apaches had gotten away with her.

It was noon the next day when the herd was delivered. Eddie Flynn, Carlos Guaderrama, Jay, and Walker Hyde were all taking a day's break from gentling the mustangs and were working on various odd jobs around the ranch when the bawling herd of a hundred or so head spilled into the lower end of the valley from the road that led down the hill. The cattle, apparently knowing they were home, trotted a ways into the open, spread out, and went to grazing. The drovers—four of them—rode directly up to the ranch house, climbed down, slapping dust from their clothing, and went inside—without even knocking, Jay noted.

From the dumbfounded looks on the faces of Eddie, Carlos, and Walker, Jay knew they were just as surprised as he by the arrival of these cattle.

"What the hell's going on?" Eddie Flynn said, burying the blade of his double-bitted ax in the chopping block.

"Whose cattle are those?"

"Reckon they must be Mr. Mac's, from the look o'

78

things. Unless somebody's just passin' through and stopped to graze and water 'em here.''

"Nobody's gonna drive cattle up that twisting, steep road just passin' through."

The four of them stood and watched the silent house for several minutes without talking.

Finally, the front door opened and the drovers came out, followed by Clyde McPherson. They paused for a few minutes on the porch, talking, and then the four strangers mounted up and rode down toward the stream at the lower end of the valley to water their horses before riding away.

Clyde McPherson saw his men standing near the corral. He came down off the porch and walked over to them. "Boys, I thought this scruffy herd we got scattered around here needed a little new blood, so I arranged to buy a few head. These cattle are a little tamer than some o' the wild longhorns we got roaming around this valley and hills." He grinned. "We'll get to putting our brand on 'em directly. We might be a while doing it, but I think we got the makings of a better beef herd here with some of these shorthorns."

Before anyone could reply, the tall rancher turned and strode back to the house.

Jay knew next to nothing about the ranching business. But he had wondered a few times since he had come here how this man could support himself, a daughter, and pay three hands and a cook on the income from the sale of a few horses. Maybe Clyde McPherson was just a wealthy gentleman rancher who only played at ranching, paying the bills out of his own private wealth. And Walker Hyde had said that Karen was in private school back in Tennessee. That had to be expensive. And then there was Randolph, the wayward son Hyde had mentioned, who borrowed money from his father to gamble. What had McPherson used for money to pay for this herd? Maybe he had gotten the cattle on credit. Jay was no businessman. In fact, he knew very little about his own father's brickmaking and construction business. The fact that business interested him even less than bricklaying was the main reason he had left home.

He shook his head. It was all a mystery to him. But then, it really was none of his concern, either. Out of gratitude for his rescuing Karen, and with some danger to his employer, he had been hired to do a job, and he might as well keep his mind on doing it for however long it lasted.

Just then the cook came out the back door of the house and began clanging the iron triangle to announce the midday meal.

# CHAPTER 11

EXCEPT for riding among the new cattle to look them over, the four men of the McPherson ranch did nothing with the herd the first few days. The animals seemed content to graze on the luxuriant grass of the small protected valley. And there was plenty of cold fresh water to drink from the pond and the ever-flowing stream.

"They're not wild cattle," Carlos remarked after an on-foot inspection of a number of them. "I sure never could've gone among 'em afoot if they were. Not like some o' those longhorns. They've got their left ears notched in a strange way. Don't recognize that mark from anything I've ever seen in the territory. Eddie, any beef down Texas way notched like that?"

Flynn shook his head, leaning forward on his saddle horn. "Nope. None that I've ever seen. Course they could've come from some other part o' the state."

"Don't make sense," Carlos continued. "They haven't been driven that far lately. Got too much flesh on 'em."

"Could've brought 'em by the railroad to Tucson," Eddie opined. "But I doubt that. Texans generally brand their cattle. Those critters ain't got nary a mark on their hides."

"If he bought 'em for breeding stock, they don't

look all that good to me," Carlos said, remounting his horse.

"Maybe they were the best he could afford," Jay suggested. "Or he bought 'em sight unseen."

Both men turned to look at him, and Jay cringed inwardly, thinking he had said something stupid. But their looks were more thoughtful than scornful, and they said nothing.

"We'd best be gettin' back to work, instead o' wondering about these here beeves," Flynn said finally, pulling his horse's head around. "We'll be busy brandin' 'em soon enough, I reckon—soon as the boss takes a notion he wants it done."

McPherson had set the following Monday as the day he wanted to start driving the newly broken mustangs to Fort Bowie. So the four men had had only a few days to knock the rough edges off the animals and get them into something like decent saddle stock for the troopers. Consequently, Jay, Eddie, Carlos, and Walker had begun spending as much time riding these mustangs as they could—up and down the valley and on the roads and trails in the hills surrounding the ranch.

And this afternoon was no exception. "I'm getting to be a regular wrangler." Jay laughed as his loop settled over the head of a mustang on his first throw later that afternoon.

"Lightnin', you got the makin's of a first-class hoss wrangler," Hyde agreed. "But I 'spect you're gonna do a lot better than that before you're done.

"Ain't this the brute that busted you in the nose that first day?" Hyde asked as he held the horse for Jay to saddle.

"Sure is. Glad he broke before I did. Think I'll let him stretch his legs on one o' these back trails today. Get him used to something besides this valley. We're about to wear a track around this place."

"Mr. Mac is lettin' us knock off early this evenin',

since it's Saturday. You goin' into town with the boys tonight?''

Jay shook his head. ''Wish I could. I can't go anywhere in public around here. Too much chance I'll be recognized.''

''They're just goin' down to Lochiel.''

''Too close to Washington Camp. Those mining towns really boom on Saturday nights. Not just local folks. Everybody from the surrounding hills comes in to dance and raise hell. You have a drink for me. I'll be sticking close around here.''

''Lightnin', I'm long past that foolishness. Besides that, a black face ain't a welcome sight to some o' those likkered-up miners. I don't want no trouble. I got me a lady friend up to Tombstone. I goes to see her now and again. That's enough socializing for me.

''Tell you what, if you're back in an hour or so, I'll take you on in a game o' hoss shoes for a quarter a game before supper.''

''You gotta be the best horseshoe pitcher in the territory, but you got a deal,'' Jay replied, grinning at the black man's look of feigned innocence. He gave the cinch a final tug and dropped the stirrup back into place.

''See you after a while.'' He put his toe in the stirrup and swung himself up. The mustang jumped and crowhopped around.

''Ah, feeling a little frisky today, are you?'' Jay pulled the animal's head around. ''You just haven't been ridden for a while.''

The mustang began to pitch, but Jay spurred him into a long lope that led out the lower end of the valley toward Mowry and on down to Patagonia. He glanced over at the ranch house as he rode by. Karen McPherson was sitting in the rocker on the porch, taking the afternoon sun, as was her daily habit now. But she was as still and expressionless as a stone statue, Jay noted sadly as he rode on past without waving. He was sure she never saw him.

He let the mustang run off his excess energy.

"Not used to being penned up, are you?" Jay yelled into the wind that whipped past his face. He could feel the animal's powerful muscles working beneath him as they followed the curving road through the low trees. "You'll get plenty of exercise soon enough on those long scouts with the Army."

Jay had been on this road only once before when he and Carlos and Eddie had gone to find the Mexican vaqueros with the mustang herd. He remembered it connected to the wagon road that led past the abandoned adobe buildings of the Mowry Mine complex, then wound down through the mining town of Harshaw and gradually out of the Patagonia Hills to the small settlement of Patagonia.

About an hour or so later the road finally began to level out, and Jay eased the mustang to a slow walk to cool him down. The afternoon heat was building up and seemed hotter at this lower elevation than it had at the ranch. The vegetation along the road had also changed, and consisted mostly of mesquite, with varieties of prickly pear, Spanish bayonet, and cholla scattered over the rocky soil.

Jay pushed back the old hat he had borrowed from Hyde and wiped a sleeve across his face. The road was deserted in the sunny stillness. There was no breeze. Puffs of dust were being kicked up by the mustang's hooves. Jay noted the usual afternoon thunderheads rising slowly above the Huachucas to his right as the road bent slightly more northward. He glanced at the deep blue sky overhead. A big golden eagle was soaring high on the rising thermals.

He felt himself getting drowsy. But he knew he would do well not to get too relaxed with this horse. Hyde had warned him that not all of the wildness was taken out of these mustangs when they were broken.

"They're just liable to jump out from under you when you ain't payin' 'em no mind," Hyde had said. "They're just lookin' to catch a man off his guard. Had one do me that way once. That critter took off with a good saddle and bridle. We never did see him again.''

Jay chuckled to himself at the recollection. ''You're gonna make some soldier a good, strong mount if he lets you know who's the boss.''

''Jay McGraw, as I live and breathe,'' came a voice from the mesquite, almost at his elbow. Jay recoiled, jerking the reins, as a cold chill went up his back. The mustang danced in a circle, fighting the bit.

''Don't reach for that gun,'' came the voice again as a figure stepped into the open. Jay's hand froze on his gun butt where it had gone automatically. His stomach felt like lead as he stared into the eyes of Tige Taggert, Sheriff Dawson's nephew. The black bore of a .45 was leveled directly at his midsection.

Jay removed his hand slowly from his Colt and tried not to make any sudden moves as he quieted his horse.

''I'd be obliged if you'll just step down off o' there,'' Tige said.

Jay did as he was told. He stood with his hands at his sides, holding the reins in his left hand.

Tige moved around to face him directly, keeping his gun steady. Jay tried to see his eyes under the shade of the hat brim. Was there any tensing around the mouth, any tightening of the trigger finger, any indication at all that this man was going to shoot him without another word? He knew Tige to be a man of violent temper. Jay resolved to do nothing to antagonize him for the moment.

''Taken to talking to your horse, have you?'' Tige sneered.

For a moment Jay didn't know what he was referring to. But then he remembered he had been idly talking aloud to the mustang when Tige appeared. A sarcastic retort leaped to his tongue, but he bit it back. ''Helps keep him quiet. He's just been broke,'' Jay replied conversationally.

''We haven't seen each other for a spell,'' the muscular

man continued. "I believe I was escortin' you to the privy when you decided, right suddenly, that you didn't have to go after all."

Jay almost laughed out loud, but managed to keep a straight face when Tige remained grim. No sense antagonizing the man further.

"Led us a merry chase, you did. I kinda figured you was hid somewheres at McPherson's ranch. I told the sheriff if we kept an eye on that place, we'd probably find you sooner or later. And sure enough, here you are." He grinned evilly under his mustache. "Fact is, I did most o' the watchin' myself from back in the trees. Weren't no trouble atall. Once I spotted you the sheriff didn't want to waltz right in and arrest you, 'cause it seems you had gone and made a downright hero of yourself after that dust-up with those Apaches when you rescued McPherson's daughter. Oh, yeah, word o' that got around these hills," he went on at the look of surprise on Jay's face.

"But now, it seems, you are about to disappear while out riding. But then your friends that hid you will find out that you're back in jail at Washington Camp. The judge is due to ride down in three days, and then you'll go on trial for killin' that poor little boy. They'll put you away for manslaughter." He grinned again. "And you thought you was so high and mighty, just waltzin' into town and tryin' to take my girl. I might just scuff you up a bit before we get down t' the jailhouse. Say I thought you was tryin' to escape the custody of a duly constituted deputy sheriff." With his free hand he pulled back his vest to reveal the small star pinned to his shirt.

Jay felt a sinking sensation in the pit of his stomach.

Tige grinned again. He was obviously enjoying himself.

While the young man had been talking, Jay had been only half listening. His eyes and mind had been busy searching for some means of quick escape. He couldn't let himself be taken back to Washington Camp. There would be nothing Tige would like better than to get him alone on one of these back trails and beat him half to death—or shoot an "escaping prisoner." Justice and the law, in spite of the badge, was a sham. Vengeance was his aim.

Jay knew he had to make some sort of move before Tige got around to disarming him. But what? He could easily get himself killed on the spot. He tried to maintain a casual, relaxed look, but his mind was racing.

A tiny movement caught his eye about fifteen yards away and behind his captor. Some small desert animal, he thought, as he tried to focus on it. There it was again. A small head poking up from a hole in the ground. It was too small to be a badger, and it didn't look like a ground squirrel. Jay casually edged around to where he could get a better view. The head moved. It was a burrowing owl. He lost interest. Nothing that he could use for a distraction to give him time to jump behind his own horse and jerk his Colt. But then a sudden thought occurred to him, and his heart began to race. He had been introduced to burrowing owls the summer before by an old prospector in the desert east of Yuma. These birds nested in abandoned burrows of other animals and were frequently seen outside during the day. Several young were hatched in the spring and seldom strayed far from their den until they left home for good in the fall of the year. But what Jay was most intent on just now was the owls' method of warning away intruders— they made a peculiar warning cry that sounded just like a buzzing rattlesnake.

The burrow was only a few feet off the road, and Jay took a few steps in that direction, leading his horse.

"Where you goin'?" Tige demanded, thumbing back the hammer of his .45.

"Just figured it was time to be startin', if we're going," Jay replied easily, secretly hoping the gun didn't have a hair trigger.

Jay edged a few more steps along toward the burrow.

"If you ain't lost your sense of direction, Washington Camp is that way." Tige jabbed the gun barrel back the way Jay had come.

Jay's heart sank. There was no way he could get Tige closer to the burrow. He took a few more slow steps. "You won't mind if I sit down over here in the shade of this mesquite and have a drink outa my canteen before we start, will ya?" He didn't wait for an answer, but strode off the road, leading his horse. He saw the owl's head disappear down the hole. He got the canteen off the saddle and, looping the reins around his wrist, sat down in the shade.

"You're stalling. But it won't help you none. You're still gonna get what's comin' to ya."

"Then you won't mind if I have a little snort o' water," Jay replied pleasantly. "Want some?" He held up the blanket-sided canteen.

"Get up outa there. We're leavin'. Git up on that horse. Now!" Tige thrust the .45 toward him.

Jay slowly capped the canteen and got to his feet, looping the strap over the saddle horn, at the same time edging closer to the owls' burrow.

Tige yanked the reins of his own horse loose from the bush where he was tied. He followed as Jay pretended to lead his mount in a roundabout loop back to the road.

Just as Jay passed the burrow he heard a slight stirring inside the hole. Tige was right behind him, leading his own mount. Jay casually scuffed his foot over the mouth of the burrow. Immediately a buzzing noise sounded. He glanced around quickly. The noise grew louder.

"Rattlesnake!" he yelled, and jumped back.

The .45 roared as Tige fired blindly at the sound.

Both horses bolted at the loud noise. Jay jumped to get the mustang between himself and Tige. He jerked his own Colt with his right hand. He threw his arm over his mount's back and pulled the trigger blindly. The Lightning flashed and roared. The mustang lunged forward at the blast so near his head. Jay wrapped both arms around the horse's neck as the horse took off. Jay's feet were hitting the ground every few yards, and he finally vaulted up onto the saddle as the mustang bolted away.

He bent low over the horse's neck and kicked him in the ribs. A gun roared behind him, and he felt a searing hot pain run up his back. He gasped and leaned even farther over. The mustang was thoroughly spooked and was running flat out as Jay tried to find the stirrups with his toes and gain control of the reins. He vaguely heard another two gunshots behind him. He hoped none of the shots had hit his mount. If Tige caught him, it would be a fight to the finish. One of them wouldn't walk away. He didn't know how badly he was hit, but the searing pain had given way to a dull hurt and a warm, wet feeling on the left side of his back. Right now he had to get away, and this wild mustang beneath him was his only chance.

# CHAPTER 12

FOR the first mile or so Jay rode blindly, letting the mustang have his head. He followed the road, winding down toward Patagonia. He threw a glance over his shoulder and there was Tige, about a quarter mile behind him, doggedly pursuing. Jay twisted in the saddle and started to fire but then thought better of it. A waste of ammunition. Only a very lucky shot would hit anything. The pain in his back was only a stinging wetness on the surface—not the deep, dull ache that would indicate a dangerous wound.

Tige was a big man, but his horse was also bigger than the mustang Jay rode. Maybe there was a chance of outrunning him, but Jay couldn't count on that. If he reached town first, there was no help to be expected there. Any law officers or citizens would no doubt side with a deputy in pursuit of his quarry. No one knew Jay in Patagonia. No, he would have to lose his pursuer. He had done it before on foot. Could he do it now on horseback? Tige was determined, all right. He'd have to give him that much. Petty jealousy and the desire for revenge ran deep in this man. Maybe he should stop, turn, and face him, Jay thought. Let's settle it right here. Tige wouldn't be expecting it. He knows I'm hit already. But Jay had never faced a man in any kind of gun battle before, and he quailed inwardly at the thought. Would he have the guts to do it? Even if he were a better shot than Tige, could he shoot another man? Would he hesitate to pull the trigger, even to protect his own life? Even a slight hesitation on his part might prove fatal. Even if he came out on top in such a shoot-out, he would be a hunted man. The law would look on it as the murder of a peace officer in the performance of his duty. Jay could see no way out of this but to escape.

It was only about half past three; darkness was hours away. Maybe he could get around one of these curves in the road, leap off, and let his mount keep running. That would work for only a few seconds until Tige saw that he was chasing a riderless horse. Then Jay would be afoot with no place to hide except a few scattered trees.

But there was something he could try. It was desperate, but he could think of nothing else. He looked back. The running horse seemed to be gaining slightly. A bend in the road was coming up. He leaned into it, the mustang's powerful muscles working smoothly. As soon as he was well into it, he reined the mustang back and turned him abruptly off the road to his left, urging him up into the slight cover of a few mesquite trees. The mustang slid to a stop at a savage tug on the reins. Jay hit the ground running with his Colt in hand. He slid to a half-seated position on the slope where he had a clear view of the road. Cocking the Lightning, he steadied his gun hand with the other and sighted on the curve of the road. Hoofbeats grew louder, and then suddenly Tige was in sight. He saw Jay at the same time and fired from about fifty yards away. Jay winced as the slug tore up the dirt three feet from his foot. But he held his fire. The galloping horse grew larger over his barrel. Another bullet whined over his head. When the horse was about twenty yards away, Jay fired. A clean miss. He cursed himself and quickly squeezed off another shot. Tige's horse dropped instantly and pitched his rider over his head as he went down.

Jay didn't wait to see more. He grabbed the reins he had snagged in a mesquite bush, vaulted into the saddle, and spurred his mustang away from the road, over a slight hill and out of range.

An exhausted rider led his equally exhausted mount into Tombstone at two-thirty the next morning. If Jay thought he was going to sneak into a quiet town and find a place to bed down with his horse for the remainder of the night, he was sadly mistaken. The town was wide open. Drunken miners were staggering up and down the board sidewalks, yelling and singing. Music from pianos and violins was leaking into the street from the open doors of at least a dozen saloons. Two score windows and doors flooded yellow light into Allen Street. Men on horseback and on wagons were going up and down as if it were high noon. Some of the merchants were open for business, Jay noted as he stopped still and looked in awe at the scene. He knew the mines never closed; they worked men in shifts around the clock. In addition, this was Saturday night—or rather, Sunday morning.

He tugged softly at the reins, and the mustang's drooping head came up and he followed Jay slowly down the street. Several wooden buildings along one side of the street were charred ruins. The smell of burnt timbers was strong as he passed these blackened remains of a recent fire.

Odors of frying steaks and beer drifted to Jay's nostrils from the open saloon doors. His stomach growled as he realized how long it had been since he had eaten. He had struck out for Tombstone, figuring it was the closest place where he could lose himself among several thousand people. There was no going back to the ranch just now. If Tige hadn't broken his neck in that fall from his dying horse, the ranch was the first place he would look. Jay would somehow communicate with Walker Hyde and Clyde McPherson later. As of now, they might think he had stolen the mustang and ridden away—especially since all hands had just yesterday received their pay for the week.

Jay thrust his hand into the side pocket of his jeans. Two half eagles—the remainder of two weeks' pay after he had paid for a hat, a pair of boots, an extra shirt, some underwear, a comb, and some other items Carlos had picked up for him at the general store in Harshaw. It wouldn't buy much in this town, but right now he wasn't so much interested in his future as he was in a room, a bath, and a stable for his horse. First he found a stable for the mustang and took charge of rubbing down the lathered animal with some dry straw and a rag before leaving him in the care of the night-duty stableboy, who appeared more interested in dozing than in working.

Other than the clothes on his back, Jay carried nothing but his gun belt and the canteen.

"I want a room," he said at the desk of one of the less-elegant hotels in town. His own voice sounded rough and strange.

"Sign the register." The balding clerk hardly glanced up. "That'll be two dollars—in advance."

Jay handed him one of the five-dollar gold pieces, and the clerk returned his change in greenbacks.

"What the hell happened to you, mister?" the clerk asked as Jay turned away with his room key.

"What?"

"Your back, man! You been horsewhipped or sumpin'?"

Then Jay's fuzzy mind remembered the congealed blood that had stiffened the back of his shirt. He must be a sight—all bloody, red-eyed, and unshaven.

"Oh, uh . . . where's the nearest bath I can use?"

"There's a Chinese bathhouse down the street about a block. They stay open twenty-four hours a day for them miners."

Jay started toward the stairs.

"Hey, it'll cost you extra if you mess up them sheets!" the night clerk called after him.

Jay acted as if he hadn't heard him as he pushed his heavy legs up the stairs. He heard the man grumbling under his breath.

Jay found his room on the second floor. He dropped his canteen on the bed and opened the window overlooking Allen Street. The bed was inviting, but he didn't dare sit or lie down on it for fear he would not get up again until morning. He took one of the matches from the holder on the table beside the bed and struck a light to the coal-oil lamp. The room was small and plain but adequate. A small mirror was fastened to the wall above the bedside table that also contained a pitcher and a bowl. He examined his face in the mirror. He didn't really like what he saw—matted hair (his hat had been lost somewhere during his wild dash for freedom), tired eyes, stubble of dark whiskers on his lean cheeks, sunburned nose and forehead.

He gingerly slipped off his shirt, wincing as the cloth stuck to the scabbing cut on the lower part of his back. He twisted around, trying to get a look at it in the mirror over his shoulder. The bullet had left a crease up the left side of his back from the lower rib cage to near the top of his shoulder blade. It was streaked with dried blood and looked like a long lash mark, but Jay breathed a sigh of relief that it was not deeper or more dangerous. He eased his shirt back on, feeling the soreness and stiffness already beginning to set in.

He turned down the wick and blew out the lamp, locked his door, and went down to the street. It took him only a few minutes to find the Chinese bathhouse a block away on Fifth Street. As the night clerk had indicated, the place was open for business, but since no shifts were changing at the mines, and it was almost three A.M., Jay was the only customer. He luxuriated in the hot, soapy water for almost

94

thirty minutes, soaking away the soreness and fatigue. When he finally came out, white and wrinkled, he toweled off carefully. Then he reluctantly pulled on his dirty clothes.

On the way back to his hotel, he went a little out of his way and stepped into the Oriental Saloon and bought a bottle of whiskey. He paid the bartender with the last of his money and walked out of the half-full saloon wondering if he had made a mistake. He hated the taste of whiskey; it was an antiseptic for his back.

Back in his room, he clumsily poured some of the whiskey over his shoulder and grimaced with satisfaction as the alcohol burned down through the raw groove. Maybe that would keep any infection from forming, he thought as he put the bottle away, slipped out of his Levi's, and crawled wearily into bed.

But, exhausted as he was, he couldn't immediately relax. He lay on his stomach in the dark, vaguely hearing the noise from the saloons below. A slight night wind stirred the curtains at the open window. He felt low and depressed and alone. He recognized these feelings as being symptoms of his fatigue. He knew a good night's sleep would set him right. But his back pained him just enough to keep him from relaxing. And with sleeplessness came unbidden thoughts of his home in Iowa—and regrets at having left it. In his mind's eye he could see the little farm town of Vail drowsing in the summer sun. He could see the corn and oats and almost smell the fresh earth. He could hear the sleepy sound of the dragonflies near the creek that was tucked into the folds of the undulating western Iowa prairie. Sometimes in the afternoons he would stop whatever he was doing to listen to the distant wail of the eastbound blowing for the crossing just west of town.

He longed to see his parents and his younger brothers and sisters. What would they be doing now? What time was it there? It would be going on five o'clock Sunday morning there. All still asleep, very likely. Sunday was a day of rest, a day for dressing up and going to church, followed by a good dinner in the early afternoon, prepared by his mother and sisters and maybe one of his aunts who had come over to visit. There would be the delicious smells from the cookstove in the big kitchen—roast beef and fresh bread, steaming corn on the cob. He groaned at the memory. And here he was, a stranger in a frontier mining town, broke, running from the law, riding his employer's horse, and a bullet wound in his back. He had certainly seen better times in his twenty-three years.

He rolled over on his side, seeking a more comfortable position. Then he grinned in the dark at feeling sorry for himself. He brought to mind what his memory had conveniently shut out. He thought of the brutally cold winter mornings, of shivering while trying to build fires in the fireplaces to warm up the downstairs rooms of the big, two-and-a-half-story brick house. He thought of starting to work at the brickyard at daylight, and dragging home wearily to supper at dark after a long day of backbreaking labor.

And the brickyard was not only hard labor, it was dangerous as well. Burned into his memory was an incident ten years ago when Jay was thirteen and his little sister Susan was seven. She had been playing at the brickyard, about a mile from the house, watching the workmen mixing the clay one summer afternoon. A mule was harnessed to a long pole that was connected to a set of paddles mixing the gooey mass in the big circular pit. The mule plodded patiently around in a circle as the men shoveled the clay and added water to get the proper consistency.

The mule was unharnessed at six, and the men quit for the day. Jay's father and brothers came home as well. It wasn't until the bricks were formed and fired in the kiln that they would have to spend the night at the brickyard, tending the fires and keeping the temperature at the correct level.

Just as they were all washed up and coming in to sit down to supper, the family dog, Queenie, part collie and part stray, came running up onto the porch, barking and jumping against the screen door. This was unusual for Queenie. Jay, two of his brothers, and his father finally went out to see what was wrong. The dog led them back to the brickyard, where they found that Susan had fallen into the pit. She was crying and holding her head above the surface by clinging to the top of one of the wooden paddles. In the fading light his father had laid wide planks across the thick, gooey mass, and Jay, being the lightest brother, had crawled out to pull the little girl up out of the sucking, clinging clay to safety. It had been a near thing—a memory that was painfully frightening to him even now.

Jay had no interest in becoming a brick mason. And yet without a skilled trade or profession of some kind, a man was doomed to hard, unskilled labor at low wages—driving a team, working on a farm, clerking in a store. He had thought briefly of learning telegraphy so he could work as a station agent for the Union Pacific or Western Union, but had then gotten a chance to go to college and had jumped at the opportunity. There he had found football and wrestling and baseball and boxing and running. Even though he enjoyed some of his classes, he had not worked at learning as hard as he should have. If he had graduated, who knows where he would be now? He took a deep breath and tried to shake the thought from his mind. He had run out of money, but he could have found a way—somehow.

Forget what might have been. He was in Tombstone, Arizona Territory, and it was Sunday morning, the twenty-sixth day of June, 1881. He had escaped death. That had to count for something. If this was the adventure he had come west seeking, it certainly didn't look like as much fun up close.

Through the open window he heard the distant sound of shots—three, four of them. Probably from one of the saloons down the street.

In the darkest hour just before the eastern sky began to pearl with the coming day, Jay slept.

# CHAPTER 13

THE sun was high when he awoke. He stretched in bed and assessed the pain and stiffness in his back. He could stand it. And judging from past injuries he had suffered, it was about as bad as it was going to get, barring infection.

He sat up and swung his feet to the floor. A breeze was blowing in the window, saving the room from the stifling midday heat. The bedsheets were faintly crisscrossed with bloody serum from his wound, he noticed, as he stood up and padded to the window. The street was relatively quiet. A few pedestrians were abroad, both men and women. Two buggies and a man on horseback passed as he watched. The angle of the shadows indicated that it was around noon. The northwest wind brought the smell of charred wood to his nostrils. And small wonder. By daylight he could see that a good portion of one block on the north side of Allen Street had been leveled by a recent fire. He could see from the window that work had already begun on clearing away the rubble in preparation for rebuilding.

This relative lull in the noise and activity must be what passes for the Sabbath hush, he thought as he turned away from the window. He poured water from the pitcher on the table into the basin and splashed some on his face. Then he straightened out his tangle of hair with his pocket comb. He filled the basin with the rest of the water and rinsed out his blood-stiffened shirt, wrung it out, and put it on, after giving the crease on his back another dose of whiskey. The coolness of the wet shirt felt good against his skin. He pulled on his Levi's and boots and went downstairs, dropped his room key on the desk in the lobby, and went outside into the brilliant sunlight. He was distinctly conscious of his grubby appearance, but even more conscious of his empty stomach. He had not eaten in twenty-four hours. He tilted up the canteen he had brought and drained the last few swallows of tepid water.

He started down the covered boardwalk and a well-dressed couple gave him some brief, disapproving looks as they passed. Probably returning from church and heading for dinner at the Maison Doré, Jay thought. He rubbed a hand over his sunburned, unshaven face. He must look and smell like a drunk. Never before had he felt like such an outcast. Women had never before pulled their skirts aside when they passed him. It was a humbling experience.

But hunger soon drove thoughts of this from his mind. He was broke. And the only things he carried on his person besides his dirty clothes were his two-quart canteen and his gun belt. The half-empty pint whiskey bottle was stuffed into a hip pocket. He was tempted to take a shot of the stuff to ease the hunger pangs, but thought it would do more harm than good on an empty stomach. Besides, he hated the taste of the stuff.

He would have to get some money before he could even ransom his horse and saddle from the Tombstone Livery and Feed.

Food was first and foremost on his mind. He slung the empty canteen over his shoulder and looked around for a saloon or restaurant that was open. About a block away he spied a man entering the batwings of a saloon. The sign over the door advertised it as the Occidental. He pushed his way inside. Noon on Sunday was not the busiest time, and the bartender was wrestling a fresh keg into place on the back bar. He stopped to sell a bottle of wine to a well-dressed man who had entered just ahead of Jay.

"What's your pleasure?" he asked, turning to Jay.

Jay steeled himself for the reply. "You got any work I can do for a meal?"

The bartender, a big, barrel-chested man with a handlebar mustache, looked him over, sniffing at the strong odor of whiskey that clung to him. He started to wave him off, but then dropped his hand. "You sober?"

"Yup." Jay didn't feel like going into a long explanation that he had not been drinking.

The bartender frowned but said, "My swamper is out with a hangover again. I need to get this place cleaned up before I start getting busy. Tell you what—you sweep down in here, run a damp mop over the floor, clean off those tables, and I'll get you something to eat. Don't worry about those spittoons."

Jay nodded with a sense of relief and took the broom the bartender handed him.

At about two o'clock Jay emerged into the sunlight of Allen Street, feeling better than he had since Saturday morning. He was pleasantly stuffed with bread, cheese, slices of ham, and potatoes. The bartender had even thrown in a draft beer. Jay had filled up his canteen with clear fresh water also.

While he was eating, Jay had struck up a conversation with the bartender, whose name was Pat Burnett. The big man talked as he set up his bar and got ready for business. It seems he had worked as a bartender in Deadwood, Dakota Territory, during the big gold rush of 1876. But things had slowed down there in the past year, so he pulled up and drifted south to the new silver boomtown of Tombstone. Jay volunteered little information about himself but mentioned that he had come here looking for work. Burnett said that if he wanted something temporary he might try for a job helping rebuild the buildings that had been destroyed by the big fire about five days previously. Before Jay could get any more information, customers began to come in and Burnett went to wait on them. Jay finished his food and waved his thanks at Burnett as he left. Jay walked down to the livery where he had left the mustang. The animal was in a clean stall, and there was a supply of hay in back, Jay noted with satisfaction.

Jay put out his hand to stroke the mustang's neck, but the animal jerked away with flaring nostrils. Jay chuckled. "Rested up and full of life again, aren't ya?"

"Take care of him," Jay instructed the lanky, tobacco-chewing stable man. "I'll probably be in town a few days." He tried to project an air of a man with plenty of money in his pocket. But he walked quickly away, hoping the stable man would not ask him to pay some on his account.

He spent the rest of the afternoon getting acquainted with the town. Most of the businesses were closed, but a few stores, restaurants, and saloons remained open to take advantage of what trade there was on Sunday. He was wary but tried not to appear so. Anyone he saw approaching on the street, he sized up from a distance. After his encounter yesterday, he was not going to be caught off guard again. And he thought he could recognize the build and walk of Tige Taggart far enough away to avoid him. Where was Tige? The man haunted his thoughts constantly now. While at the ranch, Jay had almost forgotten about the hulking, glowering man. Then he had appeared on the trail yesterday. Jay would not underestimate him again. I should have stayed around to make sure he was out of action, Jay thought ruefully. But he was desperate to get away. As it was, he had no way of knowing if being pitched over the head of his falling horse had injured him at all. There could be a telegram at the Western Union office here in town right now asking Sheriff Behan's cooperation in arresting him as a fugitive. If Tige had been banged up in the fall, he could still guess that if Jay had not gone back to the ranch, he had headed for Tucson or the nearer Tombstone. If Tige wanted him badly enough he would eventually come searching. Jay felt sorry about shooting the horse, but it was the only way he could stop the pursuit without killing the man. Then he would have been tracked down and charged with murder.

The hot afternoon wind was picking up, blowing in from the northwest across the wide plateau that Tombstone was built on. It was just such a wind, Burnett had told him, that had fanned the fire that destroyed most of one city block. The fire had started when someone had accidentally ignited a barrel of bad liquor, which had exploded and set fire to the wooden saloon.

Dust swirled up from the street, and gusts rattled gravel against the wooden buildings. He heard a loose shutter banging somewhere.

Jay found some empty chairs on the shaded porch of the Grand Hotel and sat down to rest, kill some time, and think. For some reason, a picture of Karen McPherson invaded his thoughts. He could visualize her sitting on the porch of the ranch house, staring blankly toward the westering sun. Would she ever recover? If she didn't come out of shock soon, would her father take her somewhere to get medical attention?

And what of Walker Hyde? What would he think of Jay's sudden disappearance? Maybe word of Tige's accident would leak back to the McPherson ranch so Hyde would begin to add things up.

Jay felt an uneasiness, an urge to get up and be doing something. He felt trapped by circumstances and his own lack of direction. He got up and paced restlessly back and forth on the shaded wooden walk in front of the hotel. He needed money, that much was sure. He wanted to get a stake, and then to get out of town and head north to

Tucson, or maybe toward Santa Fe. He wished this were not Sunday so he could get some kind of job and go to work immediately. It bothered him that Walker Hyde and Clyde McPherson might think he had stolen the mustang and ridden off just after receiving his weekly wages. But at present there was no way he could get word to them. He leaned against one of the roof supports and stared gloomily at the nearly deserted street.

Maybe he should leave his pistol, the only thing of value he possessed, as security for his bill at the livery and ride straight back to the ranch. He turned this idea over in his mind. He would reach the ranch in time for the drive of the horses to the fort that would begin tomorrow morning. Or better yet, he could catch up to the drive as it passed north and east toward Fort Bowie. But would he know just which route they would take? He wasn't familiar with the roads and trails in this part of the territory. Yet he had found his way to Tombstone in the dark, hadn't he? If nothing else, he could ride directly for Fort Bowie and wait for the boys to show up with the horses.

He thought again of parting with his Colt Lightning to redeem his mustang from the livery. He slid the pistol out of its holster and looked at it. Clyde McPherson had given this to him in gratitude for Jay's saving his daughter. No, he would not part with it, even temporarily, to get his horse. Temporary arrangements had a way of turning into permanent ones. Besides, he might need this weapon before he got back here to pay the livery bill. He jammed the gun back into the holster.

There was only one way. He would wait until dark and then steal his horse back. He could always pay for him later. Now he felt an overpowering urge to get back to his friends at the ranch. He had to find out what had happened to Tige. There was no way he could rest easy and get a temporary job in this town if he had to be constantly looking over his shoulder for the law to descend on him.

104

He smiled to himself once his mind was made up. He slung the canteen over his shoulder and walked off down Allen Street until he got to the edge of town. When he reached the road that dipped down then curved up toward Boot Hill, he found a shady spot near an adobe wall behind a shuttered store. He stretched out on the ground, out of sight of the road and partially sheltered from the wind. It was warm, but the breeze kept away the flies and dried the perspiration on his body. In only a few minutes, he was asleep, unmindful of small lizards that darted fitfully up and down the wall near his head.

When he awoke, the sun was well down in the western sky and the shadows were long. He sat up quickly and looked around to see if he had been observed sleeping in the streets like a common tramp. In this out-of-the-way place the Sunday quiet still prevailed. He uncapped his canteen and took a good swig of the lukewarm water. Then he stood and stretched mightily. He wished he had a mirror so he could examine his back. He leaned back gingerly against the corner of the wall, pressing carefully on either side of the long gash. It was not unduly sore. A good sign. The torn shirt he had rinsed would keep most of the dirt from the wound. It seemed to have scabbed over nicely. He still had about a half-pint of whiskey stuck in his pocket, but decided against using any more of it on his back now.

He walked back to the Occidental. Lamps were being lighted in the saloons along the street.

Burnett turned around just as Jay approached the bar. "You still looking for work?" the big man asked before Jay could say anything.

Jay nodded.

"My swamper still hasn't shown up. Here, finish trimming those lamp wicks and fill 'em with coal oil."

Jay nodded and got busy. A few customers were drifting

in—mostly a few miners, and some better-dressed men who could have been ranchers or businessmen. As Jay worked, he kept an eye on everyone who entered the batwing doors. He was not going to be caught off guard again.

But he saw no one he recognized this night.

He finished with the lamps, washed his hands, then put out a large wedge of yellow cheese and a loaf of hard-crusted bread, a knife, and jars of pickled eggs and olives on one end of the bar for the customers to help themselves.

Then came the distasteful chore of washing out the cuspidors out behind the building. Finally Burnett temporarily ran out of chores for him to do and seemed satisfied. Jay got a plate and loaded it up with food and sat down near the back of the room to eat—cold boiled potatoes, hard-boiled eggs, fried ham, and a mug of beer.

He felt good when he finished.

"Thanks," Jay said, waving to Burnett as he headed for the door.

"I'd give you a regular job as my swamper, but it doesn't pay much." Burnett grinned, drawing off a mug of beer.

Jay smiled and went out into the darkness. He paused just outside the door for a few moments to let his eyes adjust to the dimness. His best chance to steal his mustang from the livery stable would be sometime after midnight. He would have a few hours to kill.

As he leaned against the wall next to the window of the Occidental, he again felt like a cheap horse thief by planning to steal the McPherson mustang. He had never in his life failed to pay his bills, and he fully intended to pay this one—but not right now. He had to have that horse, and he was broke. That was the story. He wanted to join up with the boys from the ranch as they drove the other broken mustangs to Fort Bowie. He had to let them know what

106

had happened to him, and maybe find out what had happened to Tige.

Time dragged. He had more than four hours to kill before midnight, he noted as he glanced in the window of the Occidental at the pendulum clock on a shelf behind the back bar. He fidgeted. Finally he strolled up and down the street, forcing himself to look closely at the closed stores and the burned-out buildings. He wound up back at the Occidental, the saloon that seemed to be doing most of the business on Allen Street. He had no money; he couldn't even buy a beer or get into a poker game to kill some time. He stepped inside the saloon and noted that the hands on the clock had only crawled another twenty minutes while he had been gone.

To hell with it. He'd try the livery now. He wouldn't wait for the wee hours of the morning. How much business could the place be doing on a Sunday night as quiet as this? The owner might even have left the kid in charge who was there when Jay rode in at two-thirty this morning. It already seemed like two days ago.

He went outside without Burnett seeing him, since the big man was busy serving customers at the bar.

Keeping to the shadows, and walking casually so as to attract no notice from the few men on the street, Jay went around the block and started toward the Tombstone Livery.

# CHAPTER 14

THE big wooden livery appeared deserted in the moonlight. Jay stopped in the deep shadow a hundred yards away on the opposite side of the street and observed it. The building took up a large lot, the second from the corner of a block, next to the Wells Fargo corral. It was on the block that contained Hop Town, the Chinese quarter. The Tombstone Livery and Feed was a deep building, running back from the street, abutting another wooden building on one side and the open Wells Fargo corral on the other. The big sliding doors stood open, as usual. The night was cooling down some, but it was still very warm.

He watched the building for a good five minutes. A light buggy passed down the street, the horse's hooves kicking up clumps of dust. The ominous quiet settled in once more. The tinkle of a piano came from a saloon somewhere down the street. And still Jay waited. What was to be his plan? He saw no one on duty, but he knew someone was probably seated inside, likely dozing in a chair, since he saw no light. Or whoever was in charge might have taken advantage of the quiet night to go down the street for a drink.

He remembered the location of the stall where the mustang was housed and felt sure he could find it, even in the dark. He waited a few more minutes, hoping that some late-arriving traveler might stop at the livery and give him some hint if anyone was on duty there. But no one came. He finally decided he would have to try it blind.

Keeping in the deep shadows, out of the moonlight, he moved toward the big building. The double doors yawned open as a huge black hole in the silver-gray of the weathered planking. He crossed the street quickly and slid up to the opening. He heard a soft scuffing and blowing as some of the animals moved around. If anyone was here, he must have left the stable temporarily unattended.

Jay walked inside and started down toward the stall he remembered. A strong smell of ammonia and manure smote his nostrils. He padded slowly forward, his arms extended, feeling for any obstructions. It was right along here, on the left, he thought, straining his eyes to catch any glimmer of the interior from the outside moonlight filtering in. But except for hearing and smelling the horses close by, he could make out almost nothing.

*Crash!* He had tripped over a pitchfork and staggered into the side of a stall. The unseen horse whinnied and jumped back at the sudden commotion. Jay cursed under his breath.

"Who's that? Who's there?" wavered a youthful voice from the front of the livery. Someone *had* been on duty—most likely just awakened.

Jay fumbled for the latch on the stall door and yanked it open. A big animal nudged him aside and trotted out. As Jay reached for him, he knew instantly it wasn't his mustang. He could see the horse's silhouette in the moonlight from the door and knew the body was much too big.

Just then a lantern flared near the entrance and Jay caught the glint of a pistol in a man's hand. In desperation, Jay ran back to the next stall, recognizing his mustang in the dim light.

"Hold it right there, mister!" the boy yelled as Jay

109

yanked the latch open. A gun roared and Jay hit the ground.

"Damn fool's going to shoot one of these horses!" he grunted.

Another blast from the pistol and Jay saw that the boy was shooting at the ceiling. But the lantern was bobbing toward him. Jay grabbed at the stall door again.

"I said *stop*!" The voice cracked slightly as its owner tried to yell.

Jay ignored him. The door finally swung wide.

"Okay, horse thief, I warned you!" The weapon roared again, and the slug buried itself in the wood of the stall door. Jay sprang inside and grabbed for the mustang's mane. But the startled mustang leapt away from him and charged outside, knocking Jay against the wall. The mustang, sensing freedom, charged toward the open door, and Jay saw the lantern lurching as the boy tried to get out of the way.

Jay took advantage of the distraction and made a dash for the back door of the stable. But he stepped into a full bucket of water and went sprawling, drenching himself and twisting his ankle. He rolled quickly erect, but the bucket remained stuck on his foot.

The gun roared again, lending Jay the surge of energy he needed to sprint out the back door of the stable, pain shooting from his ankle with every step. He had never run with a bucket on his foot before. It seemed as if he were running with a peg leg, but he clumped out the back in good time nonetheless, with the stable hand shouting after him. As Jay rounded the building he thought the sound of the shouting voice seemed louder and more assured.

"Probably getting brave since he knows nobody is shooting back at him," Jay muttered to himself as he vainly tried to kick the bucket off his boot. He stumped his way across the lot behind the stable to the next street. Then, glancing about to make sure nobody was stirring, he sat down on the ground and worked his boot off. Holding the boot by its ears, he banged it sharply against the corner of a nearby privy until the bucket came loose and clanged away. He quickly slid the boot back on and jumped up, just as more shouting came from the direction of the livery, followed by two or three lanterns.

"Damned hoss thief! He run off two of my animals. I got off a few shots at him," came the youthful voice.

"He's probably long gone by now," a deeper voice answered. "We'll get a couple of the boys and help you round up your horses. A couple of us can scout around to see if we can see him." This last was said with little conviction, it seemed to Jay. Nevertheless, he opened the privy door and ducked inside, holding his breath at the stench. He held the door open a crack to breathe and to watch as two lanterns came bobbing along, illuminating two pairs of legs. They poked around halfheartedly in a woodpile nearby and looked around the corners of several buildings that Jay took to be Chinese homes, here in Hop Town. He knew the Chinese were good workers and good citizens, but they were very clannish and kept strictly to themselves. They would not open their doors in the middle of the night to get involved in any hunt for a thief, or get mixed up in any of the many drunken shooting scrapes this town was becoming famous for.

The two searchers quickly gave up and went back to the livery. Jay guessed the stableboy's shooting had attracted several men from the saloons, and maybe a deputy. He slipped out quietly and made his way several blocks west and south, keeping to the deep shadows and out of the moonlight. His Levi's were still wet from the full bucket. He was disgusted and tired, and his ankle was still a little sore as he slumped down in the doorway of a storage shed near the edge of town to try to sleep. But then he thought back over the scene in the livery. A smile came to his face, then a grin. Finally, he laughed out loud in the moonlight. The scared stableboy, and him running with his foot in a bucket—it would have made a good scene for a stage farce.

He leaned his head back against the doorjamb. He was fortunate it was still at least eighty degrees. His wet clothes wouldn't bother him that much. Before he realized how tired he was, he was asleep.

Jay awoke, chilled in the predawn darkness, and spent the rest of the night until sunup walking some warmth back into his cold, hungry body.

The sun came up and quickly began to heat up the town. The streets were filling with people.

Jay returned to the burned-out buildings along Allen Street and looked up the foreman of a crew of laborers clearing the charred timbers and pulling down the few remaining sections of blackened walls.

"Sure. Sign your name on this notebook and go to work. We can use all the help we can get."

Jay took the pencil and signed as the big foreman looked him up and down. "We're paying three dollars a day," the big man said. "Work ten hours. Half hour for lunch. Pay in cash at the end of each day. My name's Bill Martin, and what I say goes."

"Just the kind of job I'm looking for," Jay replied, handing back the pencil and notebook.

Jay was assigned to work with a man who appeared to be a Mexican but had a strong Aztec look about him, with bronzed skin and a hooked nose. Jay introduced himself and stuck out his hand, but the man just grunted and nodded, never changing expression.

"Suits me," Jay muttered, stooping to pick up a chunk of blackened timber. The men were throwing the burnt wood into two mule-drawn wagons lined up in the street.

By noon Jay was soaked with sweat and his back was growing tired from the constant bending. Most of the other dozen workmen were wearing hats and gloves. When the foreman called the lunch break, Jay breathed a sigh of relief and headed for the Occidental. He told Burnett where he was working.

"Have a beer on the house," the bartender said with a grin, drawing off a foaming mugful and sliding it across the bar.

Jay wiped a soggy sleeve across his brow and gratefully tipped up the beer, draining half of it at one gulp. "Thanks," he gasped, lowering the mug.

Burnett glanced critically at Jay's sunburned face and motioned toward the end of the bar. "Get yourself something to eat."

"Reading my mind."

"It's free to everybody," Burnett replied, moving away.

While Jay helped himself to a boiled egg and a piece of bread and cheese, he picked up a discarded newspaper that lay on a nearby table. He was startled by a front-page article that caught his eye: "President Garfield Clings to Life; Condition Slightly Improved." He scanned the column and discovered that the President of the United States had been shot several days before by an assassin and was lingering near death. Jay shook his head. He munched the bread and cheese and pondered how out of touch he had been of late. Things were going on in the rest of the country that he knew nothing about. He dropped the copy of *The Nugget.* He wondered again how his own family was faring back in Iowa.

The rest of his workday was more of the same—hot sun, sweating under the scrutiny of the foreman, hauling, lifting, sweeping, shoveling, dust and blackened grime flying around on the breeze and sticking to sweating skin.

Jay's hands were raw and his face and nose were red from the sun by the time Martin called a halt at five-thirty and paid off the laborers one by one, marking the amount by each man's name as he filed by the tailgate of a wagon the foreman was using for a makeshift table.

Jay again adjourned to the Occidental, this time paying for his beer and some food. Burnett didn't say much, but Jay knew he was reading his situation easily.

"My swamper's gone for good," the burly bartender remarked casually as he set up drinks for two men leaning on the bar next to Jay. "If you've a mind, I could use a man who's reliable. You gonna be around for a while?"

Jay agreed to do some cleaning up, but in exchange for a cot in the back room of the saloon.

After he had eaten, Jay found a clear creek outside of town, and, as the sun was slanting down toward the distant mountains, he luxuriated in a cool bath. Things were finally beginning to look up, he decided. It appeared he was stuck in Tombstone for now, but he had begun to scratch his way back. It might take him a week or so to get himself in a position to get back to the ranch, but as he watched the shadows of the bushes growing longer on the creek bank, he began to feel good about himself. At least he no longer felt like a bum.

Jay thought he had worked himself into good condition for hard labor by breaking wild mustangs on the McPherson ranch, but the next week of hard manual labor toughened him even more. He grew ever leaner and harder, his hands cracked and callused, the muscles in his arms and shoulders and back like whipcords. His stomach was flat and hard, since he ate only once a day; he estimated his weight was probably down to about 165 from his normal 173. The bullet crease on his back was healing into a long, livid scar. He kept the scar covered from his fellow workers and from the sun with a new cotton shirt he bought with the first of his wages. And the next things he bought were a hat and a pair of gloves. He was careful of his three dollars daily pay, trying to save as much as possible. At the end of the first week he was able to bail out his mustang from the livery and picketed him behind the Occidental at the suggestion of Burnett. He kept his saddle under his cot in the back room of the saloon.

It would take only a few more days and the rubble of the burned-out buildings would be cleared. Even now, other workmen were busy rebuilding the businesses where the ground had been cleared. At any time now, Jay reflected, sitting in the Occidental as darkness came on outside one evening, he could saddle his mustang and ride on back to the ranch. But his job would last no more than a few more days, anyway. So he decided to stay with it until the foreman cut him loose.

"Gonna stick around for the big doin's on the Fourth?" Burnett inquired, flinging a towel over his shoulder and coming around the bar to pick up some empty glasses left on the tables. The saloon was nearly empty just now during the dinner hour.

"The Fourth?" Jay was perplexed, trying to think what he meant.

"The Fourth of July, man! It's tomorrow. You won't be working." Burnett looked at him with mock seriousness.

"Guess I've just lost track of time. What's going on?"

"Well, the politicians are gonna have some long-winded speeches, naturally. But besides that, there's a big town picnic planned with some horse races, footraces, boxing matches, and lots of stuff. You need to stick around. You been lookin' too serious. Time to loosen up and have some fun."

The mustachioed bartender glanced around and lowered his voice. "Look, son, I haven't asked you any questions about yourself. You've been square with me, and I appreciate that. If you're on the run from the law or someone, it's none of my affair. It's your business."

"Thanks." Jay hesitated. "I gave you my right name. It's nothing really serious. But if anyone comes in here asking about me, I'd appreciate it if you didn't know anything about me."

Burnett nodded. "As a bartender, I get a lot of practice keeping my mouth shut." The barrel-chested man turned up the nearby lamp. "That still don't mean you can't stick around and enjoy the festivities, kinda quiet-like. I plan to. In fact, I plan to have a go at that prize money for fightin' that big Cornishman."

"Who?"

"Arthur Trelawney. He's a miner. Giant of a man who was in the prize ring some in the old country. Every time there's any kind of holiday or celebration around here, he gives five-to-one odds against anyone beating him in a stand-up fistfight. Could put up twenty bucks and make myself a hundred."

"If he's that good, you could be out a double eagle and get a good beating on top of it," Jay said.

"Maybe. He's nearly a head taller than I am, but I know a thing or two about defending myself. I'd like to see what I could do against him."

Jay shrugged. "I may stay around and cheer for you, then. Maybe put a few dollars on a side bet, if I get good odds."

"Well, there's cash prizes for footraces, horse races, and some other stuff, too."

Jay's attention perked up. "Cash prizes for footraces, you say? How much?"

Burnett glanced at him curiously as he went behind the bar and started washing some glasses and plates in a tub. "Can't rightly say. It varies. They charge a small entry fee, but the city puts up some of the money, along with some of the banks and mining companies. The banks, mainly. Good advertising, and it makes people think they're public-spirited and all that. Why? You thinkin' of winnin' yourself some cash?"

116

"Why not? Sure beats hard labor for three dollars a day."

"Or sweepin' a saloon for bed and board," Burnett said with a grin.

# CHAPTER 15

"**R**UNNERS, go to the mark!"

Jay hopped up and did several quick, jogging steps, lifting his knees high. His stomach started to churn. He approached the line that had been drawn in the dirt across the width of Allen Street. Crowds of people jammed the boardwalks on both sides of the street and on the flat roofs of several buildings. Faces looked out at second-story windows, and figures lined the railing of a veranda on the second floor of a hotel.

Jay walked up to the line and glanced down the empty street. The figures of several officials about two blocks away stood ready to declare the winner of this footrace. Even though he couldn't see it, Jay knew that two men held a string stretched between them across the street.

Eleven other lean young sprinters were stretching and jogging up and down behind the starting line. Jay ignored them. He had sized them up earlier and knew he had some strong competition from at least two or three of them. But he concentrated now on quelling the uprising in his stomach. It was always the same before any kind of a contest. He lined up second from the right, about eight feet from an official starter who was dressed in a waistcoat but was tieless in deference to the sweltering heat of the holiday.

Jay had shed his shirt. He was dressed only in his worn Levi's and a pair of soft but thick Indian moccasins he had bought for two dollars from his half-breed working partner a few days earlier. Jay had not had time to see if he could run well in these, but at the last minute had wet the footgear and laced them tight with rawhide in hopes they would conform closer to his feet.

He had paid his hard-earned $5 entry fee for this race and felt he had a good chance of taking the first prize of $100. The second finisher would receive $50. After paying his entry fee, Jay had had only $11 remaining to his name. He had placed $6 of that on a side bet on himself, but could get only two-to-one odds. The favorite everyone was talking about and was betting on was a whip-thin, brown Mescalero Apache who went by the English name of Rabbit. He was pigeon-toed, bandy-legged, and looked like anything but a sprinter. And most Apaches were known for their endurance as distance runners. But those who could be trusted, including Burnett, had declared that he had the most explosive start they had ever seen in a runner. He demoralized opponents. His reputation was such that it was almost impossible to get an even bet on him with anyone other than some stranger from Tucson or farther away. It was said that he showed up from out of the desert every time a footrace was held for money anywhere in the southern territory, ran and won, collected his prize, bought a bottle of whiskey, and disappeared at a trot into the desert again. No one knew where he went or where he lived. Efforts to follow him on horseback had been futile. It had been verified that he was not a reservation Indian, so it was assumed that he was either one of those rare loners or ran with the hostiles. Burnett told Jay that no one had ever heard him speak a word of English, even though it was suspected he knew some. It was also suspected that, besides winning the white man's money and making some of the best white runners look foolish, his hands were red with the blood of many white ranchers and travelers he had helped rob and murder.

But it was his prowess as a runner that concerned Jay now as he purposely lined himself up alongside this red streak. He wanted to be able to see him out of the corner of his eye without turning his head. The Rabbit was dressed only in a breechclout and moccasins. A white cotton head-band held back his long, straight black hair.

Most of the runners simply walked up and toed the mark with one foot and stood waiting for the starter's gun in a half crouch. But Jay had been coached as a runner in college and got down in a crouch with his fingers just touching the line in the dirt. The Indian crouched low, leaning forward at the waist, but held his bent arms forward, the weight of his body over the balls of his feet.

"Get set!" The perspiring official raised the six-gun over his head. Jay brought up his rear end and looked down the long, empty street.

*Bang!*

Jay burst out, arms pumping, legs driving. He had gotten the jump on the Indian. No one was in his field of vision. Thirty yards, forty yards. Then Jay was aware of someone coming up on his far left. Then the Indian began edging up on his right.

A surge of adrenalin gave Jay added speed. He flew down the street. The runner somewhere on his left fell back. But Rabbit kept coming. Jay gave it everything he had to hold him off. He heard nothing, saw nothing but the blur of buildings and people that walled them in on either side. His feet rebounded lightly from the packed dirt. The figures holding the string at the finish line were fast approaching. But the Apache was edging ahead. Jay's heart and lungs were bursting with the effort, but he couldn't will his legs to move any faster. He lunged for the string. But the Indian broke it a half step ahead of him.

A wave of noise from the crowd washed over Jay as all

the runners gradually slowed to a walk. Two of the sprinters sprawled, spent, in the dust. Bystanders spilled into the street. Jay leaned over, hands on knees, and blew hard as sweat dripped from his nose. Then he straightened up and looked around for the man who had beat him. Rabbit was jogging easily toward the shaded table where the black-hatted officials stood in consultation. Jay saw them say something to Rabbit, then hand him some greenbacks. The Apache shook his head and made some vehement signs. One of the officials grew beet red, put the money back, and reached into his pocket and drew out some coins. The sun glinted off gold as the double eagles were handed over to the victor.

The crowd began to mill around, and Jay saw money changing hands among the spectators as side bets were settled. He walked a few steps and leaned over again, laboring to get his breath. His own bet on himself to win was lost. But the $6 loss and the $5 entry fee would be well offset by the $50 he had just won in second-place prize money. But $39 was not enough. He had hoped to win much more.

Then Burnett appeared at his side, slapping him on the back. "Great race. You got second."

Jay nodded. "Rabbit had too much for me . . . down the stretch. I got a little bound up," he panted. "Shoulda cut off these jeans . . . but they're the only pair I've got."

He took his shirt, which Burnett had retrieved, and mopped his sweating face with it. "I had a regular pair of running shoes, but I left 'em at home when I came out here. Maybe have to write home for 'em."

He paused to breathe deeply as he began to recover. They walked toward the official's table to collect his $50 in greenbacks.

"Nice going, son," the race official said, handing him the money. "You almost beat Rabbit. Nobody's come close to doing that for a long time."

Jay muttered his thanks and pocketed the money.

"What's your name?" a voice at his side asked.

Jay turned to see a lean man with blond hair, in a collarless shirt and carrying a pencil and notepad.

"What?"

"I'm with the *Tombstone Epitaph*."

"Uh . . . Jay. Jay Miller," Jay said, giving the first phony name that came to mind.

"Where you from?"

"I'm working here now, but I'll be leaving shortly," Jay said, trying to ease away.

"You're really fast. Have you done a lot of running before? Are you from somewhere back east?"

"I've done a little running," Jay replied quickly. "I have to go now."

"Wait. I think our readers would want to know a little more about you," the man yelled after him. Jay just shook his head and waved as he slid into the crowd on the boardwalk, with Burnett following.

"That's one man you want to stay away from if you're on the run," Burnett said quietly.

"I know," Jay replied, pausing to pull the cotton shirt over his sweaty torso.

"Good thing you thought to give him another name. Or is Miller your real name?" The bartender smoothed his handlebar mustache with the back of one big hand and squinted at Jay in the sunlight.

"No, Miller's not my name. . . . When are you taking on the Cornishman?" Jay asked, changing the subject abruptly.

"About an hour. He has two other challengers this time. Not as many as before, but I want to go last. If the other two can't beat him, at least they might wear him down a little."

"What do you think of your chances?"

Burnett grinned wryly. "I may look like a fat man, but

feel that." He took Jay's hand and directed it to his stomach. Jay's probing fingers felt solid muscle in the rounded midsection. He arched his brows in surprise.

Burnett grinned. "See what I mean? At least I'll have overconfidence on my side. He'll be looking to put me away with one punch in this 'soft' belly." He chuckled. He balled one massive fist and flexed his right arm. Even under the shirtsleeve, Jay could see the bicep stretching the cloth.

"Being strong and in condition doesn't necessarily make a good fighter," Jay remarked. "You ever done any fighting?"

"I've been in a few brawls in my time," the big man answered as he fell into step beside Jay. "Got a few prizefights up in Dakota Territory. Won some."

The crowd on the street was thinning as the saloons began to fill up. It was a hot day, and there were thirsts to be quenched. A man with a booming voice was yelling instructions to the participants of the upcoming horse race that was forming up in Allen Street.

"Hey, you got my money?" Jay looked up and saw the man he had placed a bet with.

"Yeah. Here's your six," Burnett answered, digging into his pocket.

"Good race, boy," the man said, "but I didn't think you could beat Rabbit. In fact, I don't think anybody can."

Jay gritted his teeth. "Maybe. We'll see. I may get another shot at him sometime."

The man just smiled as he took his money and tipped his derby. "Look me up if you want another wager," he said over his shoulder as he walked away.

"Too bad they haven't got any wrestling matches lined up today," Jay said as they pushed through the batwing doors into the cooler interior of the Occidental. "Want a beer? I'm buying for a change."

Burnett shook his head. "Not now. A drink of water, maybe." He glanced around at the crowded bar. "Too bad I'm not working today. I could pick up a lot of tips. But I stand to make a lot more fighting today."

"How much did you put up?"

"Two hundred. At five-to-one."

Jay whistled softly as he signaled one of the two busy bartenders. "You got a lot of confidence."

"If I don't believe I can win, who will?" the big man said.

"A knockdown will signal the end of a round," the lean, mustachioed referee said to the two combatants as Burnett and the Cornishman stood facing each other in a roped-off section of Allen Street just over an hour later. "The first man who can't come back to scratch within two minutes of a knockdown will be declared the loser. There will be no hitting below the belt, no kicking, eye-gouging, or biting. Let's have a fair fight. Shake hands now, and wait for the bell."

The fighters parted, and Burnett came back to the rope where Jay crouched with a jug of water and a towel. Burnett squatted and bounced up and down.

"Okay, big man, this is it. Don't try to slug it out with him. He'll try to end it with one or two punches like he did with those two earlier."

Burnett nodded, flexing his arms and shoulders.

A crowd of men and boys, eight deep, pushed up against the rope barricade that had been strung across the street just behind them.

"Clean up on him, Arthur!" a man shouted.

The big Cornishman waved to acknowledge the yell.

"Twenty dollars says he puts him away in the first round," another man said in a lower voice in the crowd behind them.

"Hell, that's no bet," a voice answered. "What odds you giving? The big Cornishman's undefeated."

Jay hoped Burnett hadn't heard. The only betting seemed to be on how long the knockout would take. There was no question about the outcome.

The early-afternoon sun beat down unmercifully. There was no breeze, and Jay noted the buildup of storm clouds in the west. The mass of humanity packed closely around them added to the sultriness of the afternoon heat. Sweat glistened on Burnett's broad forehead and big shoulders. He was stripped to the waist, revealing a barrel chest covered with a thick mat of black curly hair.

"If the wrong man wins, this crowd could get ugly," Jay commented, looking around at the men who were shouting for Burnett's quick end.

"Meaning, if I win and a lot of money is lost, I could be in big trouble."

Jay nodded.

"Don't worry. I've made some good friends in this town. I think I could count on most of them, if it came to trouble. Besides, there's our intrepid Sheriff Behan to keep things in order."

Jay followed his gaze and saw a smallish, partly balding man near the rope barrier. "He must be a lot tougher than he looks," Jay commented.

"He's got a few deputies and all that Clanton clan backing his play," Burnett said. "But I don't trust any of them—even to break up a riot. Ah, and there's Wyatt and Virgil Earp—two good gamblers. Wonder who they're betting on?"

Jay picked out two tall lean men dressed in white shirts and black hats, standing slightly above the crowd on the raised boardwalk in front of the Oriental Saloon. Each sported a sweeping black mustache. They looked a lot alike, except that Virgil's face was a little rounder. They both had the look of gamblers—or undertakers, Jay thought.

"Sure you wouldn't rather be over at Schieffelin Hall listenin' to patriotic speeches?" the bartender asked, a slight twinkle in his eye.

Jay grinned. "Just keep away from his right. He's been working a single jack so long, that right arm's as big as my leg."

Indeed the man who strode up and down impatiently a few yards away was a giant of a man. A good six feet, six inches tall, he was built like a Greek statue, wide galluses stretching over the bare, muscular torso. He had a mop of curly brown hair, ears that protruded slightly from his head, and a big lantern jaw. But more than his appearance, Jay noted the way he moved. It was not with the grace of an athlete, but with the heavy-legged stride of a laborer.

"Hell, I'm no ballerina either," Burnett answered when Jay pointed this out.

"Just keep moving to your right away from his right hand," Jay cautioned.

*Clang! Clang!*

A man on the far side of the street had struck an iron triangle.

The two fighters moved up and toed the line scratched in the dirt.

# CHAPTER 16

THE two men gripped hands briefly, and then the referee stepped away as they began to circle each other warily. Arthur Trelawney flexed his shoulders and balled his two big, hard-knuckled fists, assuming a classic boxing stance.

Burnett circled to his right, hands held high to protect his head, making a feint or two to draw a swing. But the miner stood his ground, pivoting to face his opponent but making no moves himself.

This went on for a full minute, and the crowd grew restive.

"C'mon, this ain't no goddamn dancin' match!" a drunken voice yelled.

"Fight or go home!"

"Boooo!" A bottle sailed out of the crowd and skidded across the makeshift ring. The referee kicked it to one side.

Trelawney was waiting for an opening to land his mighty right cross—the punch that had downed so many challengers before.

Finally, Big Art took a wild swing that Burnett easily dodged, but he didn't try to get inside that long reach.

Burnett was crouching and bobbing, moving to his right, conscious of the bigger man's right. But suddenly the

Cornishman's left shot out and caught Burnett in the chest. The unexpected force of the blow staggered him, and the big man moved in, flailing. Burnett covered up, but a solid smash to his left shoulder from Trelawney's right knocked him to his knees. The crowd was yelling for blood.

*Clang!*

The referee immediately stepped in to separate them as the round ended.

Jay bounded forward and helped the bartender to his feet and back to his side of the arena.

"He's got a kick like a mule," Burnett said, flexing his left shoulder. "My whole arm went numb for a few seconds."

Burnett went down to one knee to rest.

*Clang!*

The fighters toed the mark once more, then began to circle. Arthur Trelawney, looking confident now, held his fists at waist level, eyeing the burly bartender who circled him like a stalking grizzly bear.

Suddenly Burnett went in with a roundhouse right that caught the big man leaning back on his heels. The bare fist smacked into the miner's side and the crowd howled.

The miner was more irritated than hurt. He immediately countered with a whistling right that missed the ducking Burnett. Then, quicker than Jay thought he could move, Burnett was inside the long reach and pounding short, powerful jabs to the midsection. The miner was driven back as Burnett bored in. The big miner couldn't get a shot at him. Finally the miner brought down his right fist in a clubbing chop to the back of the neck, and Burnett went to his knees.

The referee rushed in as the iron triangle was struck. Round two was over.

Jay helped the wobbly Burnett to the rope barricade. "Get down on one knee and get your breath," Jay said.

128

"Rabbit punch," the bartender gritted, leaning over. "Like punching an oak tree," he panted.

"Don't talk. Just rest." He gave Burnett a sip of water.

*Clang!*

The fighters approached the center once more, Trelawney looking as fresh as when he started. They cautiously moved around, each looking for an opening.

The day was growing hotter and muggier. The light breeze had died completely, and the mushrooming clouds threatened a thunderstorm. A sheen of sweat covered the torsos of both fighters.

Burnett feinted to his left and tried to drive in to his right to get inside, but the miner swung a hard right that caught Burnett a glancing blow on the side of his head. The force of the blow was still enough to knock him down.

Back on his side of the arena, Jay spoke urgently in his ear, the noise of the crowd just behind him drowning out all other sounds. "They're not scoring points. It's a fight to the finish. So go down and end a round whenever you need a rest."

Burnett nodded but didn't try to answer as his lungs fought to suck in the hot air.

*Clang!*

Three more rounds followed, each lasting several minutes. Each ended with a knockdown of Burnett. Sweat trickled down the bartender's face as he knelt by Jay. His mustache drooped. Perspiration soaked his trousers and matted the hair on his chest into black curls. A large bruise was puffing the outside of his left eye.

Jay glanced across at the other side. The big miner was finally beginning to show signs of wearing down as well. He sat on a wooden stool his seconds had provided for him, his head down, arms hanging limp, as someone fanned him with a shirt.

"You got him now," Jay said. "You broke his spirit.

129

He's never had to go this long with anybody else. He's tired. You can take him!''

Burnett dragged his tired eyes to Jay's face but didn't answer as he fought for air, mouth agape and blood trickling from one nostril.

*Clang!*

Jay noted that Trelawney's arms and legs seemed to have gained some lead as the miner shuffled out to meet Burnett.

This time, instead of circling, Burnett drove in hard, catching the miner off guard. He whipped a right and left to the lower abdomen, the short thick arms driving the big fists like the pistons of a steam engine.

"Ugh!" The champion nearly doubled over. Any ordinary man would have been on the ground.

Obviously hurt, the miner tried to back clear and stall. The crowd was screaming, sensing a turn of this battle. Jay had to move a few feet away from a man who was yelling in his ear.

"Get him! Now! Go after him!" Jay yelled, his voice all but drowned in the roar.

But Burnett was tiring badly. It didn't appear to Jay that he had enough left to follow up his temporary advantage. But he gamely pursued. A few more blows were exchanged, but neither man did any damage, since the power had drained from their arms.

Finally they backed away from each other, arms low, gasping, eyeing each other like two huge beasts fighting to the death but neither one able to make the kill. Burnett moved in again, slowly, and Trelawney stood his ground. The miner swung the deadly right cross, but the sting had gone out of it, and Jay saw the big man wince as his fist bounced off the top of Burnett's skull. In obvious pain, the miner started to back up just as Burnett drove a weak left to the midsection. The miner bent slightly forward, still favoring his right hand. Burnett, still moving forward,

130

stepped on the big man's left foot, throwing the miner off balance.

Jay saw Burnett's shoulders bunch as he gathered all the strength he had left. He brought up a short right uppercut that exploded flush on the miner's jaw. The big man's head snapped back, his arms dropped, and he toppled backwards onto the ground like a falling redwood.

The clang of the iron triangle was lost in the roaring of the mob of spectators. The roar continued as the seconds rushed to Trelawney's aid. Burnett stood there, arms hanging at his sides, mouth open, chest heaving.

The miner did not get up, so his friends worked on him where he was. The referee stood to one side, holding his silver pocket watch in his hand. The seconds dragged by as Jay held his breath.

The miner began to move and then was helped to a sitting position. One man got under each arm and attempted to lift the giant body. But the wires were down, and the wobbly legs could not respond. The referee glanced up and then back at his watch. He held up his hand and then pointed to the man with the iron triangle.

*Clang! Clang!*

The referee stepped up and pointed down at the mark scratched deep in the dirt street. Burnett put his toe to the line.

The miner had fallen back to his knees, his head hanging down. The referee waved his arms and grabbed Burnett's wrist, raising his bloody-knuckled fist high.

*Clang! Clang! Clang! Clang! Clang!*

The wild pounding of the triangle was barely audible above the clamor of the astonished crowd that surged forward through the rope barricade. Arthur Trelawney was king no more.

Jay was carried forward as the crowd rushed in to surround Burnett. Many in the crowd were busy settling bets with each other, and several fistfights broke out.

131

Before Jay could reach Burnett's side, the bruised new hero was lifted and borne away on many shoulders. Jay was pushed and shoved and elbowed aside as he fought in vain to get close to his friend.

Suddenly, something hooked the back of his belt and he felt a pressure in his side.

"So we meet again, Jay McGraw!" a deep voice said close to his ear. A chill went up Jay's back at the familiar sound.

Tige had found him!

Jay stopped in his tracks. He knew without looking around that there was a gun muzzle in his side. He glanced quickly about for help, but he knew no one in the remainder of the crowd that was quickly dispersing. Where was that Sheriff Behan? But no, he didn't want him. This Tige Taggert was supposed to be the law too.

"You're not getting away from me this time, you slippery bastard!" the voice hissed. "You owe me for a damned good horse and a lot of bruises. Move!"

"Where?" Jay stalled.

"We're not goin' to any damn jail, that's for sure," Tige gritted. "We're goin' just far enough outa town so I can beat you to a pulp in private!"

Jay felt his blood rising. Maybe he would get a shot at fighting this man face to face, without guns. He would welcome the chance to settle this once and for all. Tige had dropped his pretense of arresting him as a fugitive. It was now just revenge, pure and simple.

A loud argument broke out nearby between a Mexican and a black man. The two drunken men began pushing each other. One staggered into Tige and Jay. Jay heard a thump, and a body slid down his legs. He jumped sideways and looked down. Tige lay at his feet, facedown in the dirt. A black face was grinning at him.

"Walker Hyde!" A wave of relief swept over Jay at the

132

sight of his friend, who stood there holstering his gun. Carlos Guaderrama was next to him.

"Hello, Lightnin'. We been missin' you down at the ranch. Wondered where you'd got to," Carlos said.

"This fella's gonna wake up with a mighty sore head shortly," Hyde said. "If you've a mind to come back, we'd best get gettin'. Got your horse tied over here. Couldn't find the saddle, though."

Jay grinned broadly through his ten-day growth of beard. "Forget the saddle; I'll get it later."

He looked up and saw the slight figure of Sheriff Behan and another man step off the boardwalk and start toward them from the opposite side of the street.

"We have company," Carlos observed at the same time. *"Vamanos!"*

The three started walking away from the prostrate Tige.

"Hold it there!" came a shout from behind them.

As one, they sprinted around the corner of the Eagle Brewery Saloon into Fifth Street and made for their horses.

# CHAPTER 17

"**I** don't know where you two came from, but I'm sure glad you showed up when you did. Perfect timing," Jay said when the three finally slowed their horses to a walk. He shifted his weight to one cheek to help relieve the pounding his rear end had taken from the mustang's backbone.

"We saw you earlier, but waited until the fight was over," Carlos said. "You looked busy at the time."

"What were you doing in Tombstone?" Jay asked. "And where's Eddie Flynn?"

"After we got the horses delivered to Fort Bowie and came back, the boss gave us a couple of days off to celebrate the Fourth. Eddie decided to go to a *baile* at Lochiel. I think he has his eye on a certain señorita who lives near there," Carlos said.

Lochiel, a border settlement named for the Scottish hometown of its founder, consisted of several adobe buildings close to Washington Camp. Its heyday as a mining town and a departure point for ore pack trains to Mexico City was long past, but it had the historic distinction of being the spot where Spanish explorers had first entered what was now the Arizona Territory.

"Like I told you before, I have a lady friend in Tombstone," Hyde added. "So I come up here to see her and take in all the holiday doin's. Carlos just decided to ride along with me."

"Wanted to try my luck at the faro tables. I even had a small bet on that big miner. Good thing we didn't stay around long enough to pay off," Carlos said, grinning.

"Mr. Mac thought maybe you done run off with one o' the mustangs. I tole him, 'No suh, that ain't like that boy. I know Lightnin' wouldn't just light out like that without a word to nobody.' And I shore knew you wasn't no hoss thief. I figured sumpin' musta happened to you. I scouted several o' the trails that evenin' when you didn't come back, but didn't find no trace. Then, the next mornin', we had to start trailin' the mustangs to Bowie."

"We thought maybe you'd be there when we got back," Guaderrama said.

"I tried to," Jay said, and then related his story, bringing them up to date on his stay in Tombstone. "I'd been on the lookout for Tige ever since I hit town, but I had no idea what happened to him until I got careless and let him slip up and stick that gun in my back just now," Jay concluded.

"Well, they ain't gonna be a place safe for you hereabouts as long as that man's on the loose," Hyde remarked. "I seen his type before. He be like a durn bulldog."

They rode silently for a few minutes as the trail dipped and rose toward the foothills of the low mountains directly ahead of them. Jay looked back over his shoulder. No horsemen were in sight, and no dust cloud told of pursuers. Satisfied that the law was not following, he turned back to the front. Behan and his deputies would be too busy keeping order in that crowd in town to bother chasing three men for slugging some out-of-town deputy in a personal feud. Even so, Jay would be glad when the scrub oaks and evergreens of the Huachucas hid them from the view of anyone on this open plateau.

135

The grilling sun had slid behind a towering bank of thunderclouds when the three horsemen dismounted to water their horses at a small clear stream in the foothills. Jay slid stiffly to the ground and held the reins as the mustang plunged his dusty muzzle eagerly into the cool water. Sweat stung Jay's eyes in the still, sultry air. It was ominously quiet, except for the burbling of the stream at their feet.

When the horses had drunk for a couple of minutes, the three men pulled them away and tied them to some nearby shrubs, where they began cropping the edible leaves within reach. Jay flopped down on his belly and thrust his head into the flowing stream. The water was bracingly cold, and he came up to take a long, satisfying drink. The other two contented themselves with scooping water up with their cupped hands and then filling their hats and pouring them over their heads.

"Whew! Boy, does that feel good!" Carlos sighed.

Jay rolled over on his back and stretched.

"We should be home by dark," Hyde mused, sweeping a look at the sky. "If'n that rain holds off."

A low, distant rumble answered him.

"Never knew it rained so much in Arizona," Jay commented. "Folks back home have the idea that Arizona Territory is just one big hot desert."

"No suh," Hyde said. "Most of it's a mighty beautiful and green land, as you can plainly see. They's some mighty hot dry spots, but that just makes the rest of it seem that much better." He smiled and a wistful look came into his eyes. Jay knew the middle-aged bronc buster had found a home he would never leave.

"Is Mr. McPherson planning on rounding up some more mustangs soon?" Jay asked as Carlos knelt on a rock to fill his canteen.

"Mr. Mac's always on the lookout for more horses," Hyde replied. "I reckon he's got those Mexican vaqueros out huntin' some right now. Long as there's a market, he'll buy 'em, bust 'em, and sell 'em.'' He paused and looked thoughtful. ''But he seems to be gettin' more and more into the cattle business, too. Maybe he thinks that's what's gonna be the future o' this territory. I don't much care for it, though. There may be more money in those poor dumb brutes, but give me a dozen good, spirited mustangs any day. Course, I ain't the boss, so I'll just hafta go along and take orders or move on somewheres else.''

''We better be movin','' Carlos interrupted, yanking his mount's reins loose.

Jay rose and vaulted onto the mustang's bare back. Their mounts splashed across the stream and took to the trail, heading southwest.

It was full dark when the three horsemen came down out of the trees into the small valley that held the McPherson ranch. Yellow light shone from the windows of the bunkhouse and the ranch house. The moon had not yet risen, but Jay could see by the starlight the dark shapes of many grazing cattle. It seemed that there were many more than when he had left here. But the cattle were only something that he absently recorded in the back of his mind. All afternoon what he had really been thinking about as they wound single-file along the rocky trail, was the dark-haired Karen McPherson. Neither Carlos nor Walker had mentioned her. Jay had started to ask about her several times, but for some reason he did not understand, he could never utter the question. Maybe he was afraid of the answer he would get. Was she still here? Was she any better? Any worse?

His pulse quickened as they neared the ranch buildings. Jay groaned as he slid off the mustang's back near the bunkhouse. Now he knew why saddles had been invented.

The bunkhouse lamp had been lighted and left burning low, but Eddie was apparently still at Lochiel.

As Jay and Walker unsaddled the horses and hobbled them before turning them out to graze, Carlos went up to the ranch house to rouse up the cook for some supper.

"They weren't expecting us until tomorrow," Carlos said, coming into the bunkhouse a quarter of an hour later with a steaming pot of beans and setting them on the wooden table. "Felipe thought he was going to have the day off." He grinned. "He wasn't too happy about having to rustle up supper, so it's slim pickin's—just beans and tortillas. Dig in, gents."

They fell to eating in silence. Jay didn't realize how hungry he was until he smelled the beans. It had been a long, tiring day. As he wrapped a tortilla around some beans he wondered what Burnett was doing now. The stocky bartender was probably basking in all the notoriety that was now his for defeating the giant miner, Trelawney. Would Burnett even wonder where Jay had gone so suddenly? Tige had been the cause of Jay's sudden flight on two occasions now. And Jay knew he would have to deal with his adversary soon to settle this once and for all, or else leave the territory altogether. Jay didn't want to flee while he was still under suspicion of killing a boy, but technically he was a fugitive from justice since breaking jail at Washington Camp. He sighed, and his shoulders sagged with fatigue. Glad as he was to be back at the Mc-Pherson ranch—a place he had come to regard as home during his short stay, he knew he could not stay here indefinitely. He knew the dogged Tige would come looking for him here as the most logical place, even though Tige had not seen who struck him from behind in Tombstone.

Before he even finished his supper, Jay felt himself nodding, and shortly after ten o'clock he sought his bunk. Walker and Carlos broke out a greasy deck of cards to play by the lowered lamplight, but the murmur of their quiet game did not prevent Jay from dropping off into a deep sleep almost immediately.

The sun was streaming in the window of the bunkhouse when Jay awoke. Walker and Carlos had let him sleep through breakfast, but he didn't care. As he slipped on his moccasins and strapped on his gun, he felt well rested. He stretched and yawned and stepped outside into the bright morning. Beyond the buildings and corrals, the lush green valley sloped up into the trees. A tranquil, pastoral scene. But now the grass was being cropped by at least four times as many cattle as had been here when he left. It looked as if Clyde McPherson was going into the beef business in a big way. Even to Jay's inexpert eye, this small valley could not support many more head.

He shaded his eyes and looked around for some sign of human life. Was everyone at the ranch house? But then he spotted several figures on foot about two hundred yards away on the other side of the creek. Jay started toward them. He crossed the small stream on the rocks and approached the men. Carlos, Walker, Clyde McPherson, and even the cook, Felipe, were all grouped around one of the steers. A fifth man stood with them, a man Jay had never seen before.

". . . first noticed it three days ago," Clyde McPherson was saying, "after I got back from Fort Bowie. Several other head are affected too. But this steer is one of the worst. I first noticed how stiff-legged and lame some of them appeared from a distance. I took a closer look and at least a dozen head had *some* symptoms, so I sent that Mexican boy to fetch you from the fort. If I'da known it when I was there, you could've ridden back with us."

Carlos and Walker Hyde nodded to Jay as he walked up and stood listening.

"Dr. John Brownlow, the Army contract veterinarian from Fort Bowie," Carlos whispered to Jay.

Brownlow, a stocky six-footer with a touch of gray in his hair, had his sleeves rolled up and was examining the mouth of the steer as Hyde held the animal by a rope around his neck. But the steer didn't seem inclined to jerk away or even move. In fact, he stood with his head hanging listlessly, eyes clouded. Saliva hung in strings from the animal's mouth.

"I saw the same thing in Mexico when I was a young man," Felipe said. "We call it *mal de la yerba*. Many of our cattle had it."

The veterinarian did not reply as he finished his examination. Jay could see the sores on the soft tissue of the steer's lips and gums that were apparently causing the excessive drooling.

Dr. Brownlow then bumped up the steer's front feet, one by one, and carefully probed around the coronary band at the top edges of the hooves. The animal stood docilely. The veterinarian then took a thermometer from his leather bag, shook it down, and pulled the animal's tail upward. As he inserted the instrument, he turned to McPherson. "Have you noticed any of these symptoms among your horses?"

"No. And at least four of our horses have been among these cattle for more than a week."

Dr. Brownlow nodded. He pulled out a silver pocket watch and held it as he kept his other hand on the end of the thermometer.

He finally extracted the slim thermometer, wiped it, and held it up. Then he slipped it back into its case and put it into his bag.

The small group watched him intently, saying nothing. Felipe Fernandez stood to one side, looking smug, as if he, with his many more years of age and experience, had correctly diagnosed the sickness of these cattle.

Dr. Brownlow took a bottle of strong-smelling disinfectant from his bag, poured it over his hands, and wiped them thoroughly on a clean cloth. Then he rolled his sleeves down and buttoned his cuffs.

"Mr. McPherson, you have big trouble here," Dr. Brownlow said gravely. "This animal is not infected with vesicular stomatitis—*mal de la yerba*, as your cook calls it. If that were the case, some of your horses would likely have contracted it. No, this disease affects only cloven-hoofed animals. The symptoms are very similar, but I'm afraid what we have here is much more serious—an outbreak of *la fiebre aftosa*—foot-and-mouth disease. Have you ever seen this disease before? No? But I'm sure you've heard of it. See these vesicles on the lips and gums here? And on the tongue?"

Jay crowded forward with the others to see the suppurating sores on the mucous membranes as the veterinarian forced the steer's jaw open.

"They make his mouth so sore he can't eat. The fever kills the appetite, and some swelling of the pharynx makes swallowing difficult. He'll lose weight and could eventually starve. And these sores on his feet may get so bad his hooves will come loose. He'll go down, and hunger and thirst will make an end of him. It's not the disease that usually kills outright; it's what it does to weaken the animal—the fever, the open sores, the secondary infections, the crippling of the joints. It often affects the heart and internal organs as well. Foot-and-mouth disease is very contagious. It spreads like wildfire. Humans are even suspected carriers."

Carlos and Walker looked stonily at each other. Jay glanced at Clyde McPherson. The rancher's face was draining of its color under his hat brim.

Dr. Brownlow picked up his bag and started walking toward the ranch house. "This will have to be reported immediately, of course. You will have to isolate your herd until we can find out if these are the only ones infected.'' The doctor stopped and turned back to see if Clyde McPherson was listening. The tall rancher stood as if transfixed, still staring ahead.

"I know this is a shock, Mr. McPherson," Dr. Brownlow continued. "I'm sorry to be the one who has to tell you the bad news. But I suppose you know that there is no cure for foot-and-mouth disease. Your entire herd will have to be destroyed. All we can do is try to stop the spread of the disease.''

McPherson shook himself out of his paralysis and seemed to collect his thoughts. "Yes, yes, of course, Doc," he replied, turning to walk with the veterinarian as the four others fell in behind them.

"The last time there was an outbreak in this country was in 1870," Dr. Brownlow was saying as he reached his buckboard and dropped his bag in the back. "We'll have to backtrack to find out where these cattle came from. I don't know where you got them, but I'd bet my reputation they're from Mexico or Central America.''

McPherson was noncommittal.

Dr. Brownlow pushed his hat to the back of his head and took a bandanna from his hip pocket to wipe his perspiring face. "When I get back to the fort, I'll wire Dr. Peterson in Tucson. All the herds in the southern territory will have to be checked—or as many of them as we can get to. We'll have to get the word out to all the ranchers. I'd suspect the territorial governor will probably close the border to all cattle imports," he went on, his thoughts running ahead as he prepared to climb into his buckboard. "If this outbreak spreads, it could ruin the cattle business in a large part of the country. We've got to stop it here—if we're not already too late. . . . Mind if I get a good drink of water before I go?''

"Uh, no, no. Go right ahead, Doc." McPherson reached

142

into his pocket. "How much do I owe you for coming out?"

"Twenty dollars ought to cover it. On second thought, to hell with it. You don't owe me anything. The Army pays me. I'm just sorry that you have to lose your whole herd. Keep your money. You'll probably need it worse than I will."

Jay and the three other men stood to one side, eyeing their boss, who still seemed to be in a state of shock.

The veterinarian capped his canteen, dropped it in the back of his wagon, climbed up, and took up the reins. With a wave of his hand he slapped the reins over the team and clattered down the road toward the trees at the lower end of the valley.

The dust of the wagon's passing was still hanging in the still, sunny air, when Clyde McPherson stirred himself. "Carlos! Saddle my roan." He turned toward the house and vaulted up the porch steps. At the door he turned back. Carlos had not moved.

"I said, saddle my horse! Damn it, move!" he yelled. Then he was gone inside.

Carlos ran for the corral.

# CHAPTER 18

JAY and Walker looked at each other. The black man compressed his lips and shook his head.

"Where's he going?" Jay asked. He felt a strange sinking in the pit of his stomach.

"Don't rightly know, Lightnin'," Hyde said. "But I'm afeared of the worst. C'mon."

Jay followed him as he jogged toward the barn, where Hyde ducked into the tack room and hauled down the boss's saddle and bridle. By the time they got back outside, Carlos had the roan roped and snubbed to the corral gate. Carlos made short work of saddling the gelding.

"I've never seen the boss in such a rage," Carlos said. "He's usually calm and in control of himself."

"I got me a bad feeling about this," Walker Hyde said.

"What's he up to?" Jay asked.

"Jay," Carlos said, tugging on the cinch, "remember when we were trying to figure out the strange ear notchings on that first bunch of cattle that came in here a few weeks back?"

Jay nodded.

"Found out through a cousin of mine that those particular ear markings are used by the ranchero of Manuel Verdugo, one of the larger spreads in northern Sonora.

And Walker, Eddie, and I believe these cattle were rustled from the Verdugo herds. We have no proof, but . . ." He shrugged. "I myself am convinced the herd that passed us that night in the Santa Cruz Valley when we were out to get those mustangs was being rustled across the line. We think these cattle are part of those from Mexico. We don't know how Mr. McPherson is involved, but I have a feeling he's going to confront somebody about these sick cattle." He glanced around as he gave the roan a pat on the rump. "I think McPherson is about to be exposed as a rustler."

Jay gave a low whistle. "You think he really knew these cattle were stolen when he got them?"

Carlos nodded. "Yeah. I hate to say it, because Mr. Mac has always treated me more than fair. But he's a smart man. He knows. He's involved somehow."

Jay glanced at Walker Hyde. The man's seamed face looked older than Jay had ever seen it. He looked as if he were about to cry. Jay had a feeling that Hyde had somehow been betrayed by a good friend.

There was a crash of glass breaking inside the house, then the sound of a muffled yell and what sounded like a girl's scream.

Jay hesitated, then jumped up on the corral to climb out.

Just as he got his leg over the top rail, the front door of the house burst open and McPherson ran out holding a carbine in one hand and jamming his hat on his head with the other. He leapt down the steps and strode swiftly toward the corral.

Carlos swung the gate open and handed the rancher the reins of his horse. Clyde McPherson slid the rifle into the boot and, without a word to any of them, jerked the horse's head around and mounted. The startled roan danced in a circle. The rancher dug in his rowels and the horse leapt forward out the gate, across the flat, and down the long sloping trail toward the woods.

The three men stared after him, not knowing what to say or do.

The drumming of the hooves died away in the distance.

"Help! Someone, please help! Walker! Carlos!" came a quavering female voice.

Jay's head jerked toward the house. Karen McPherson was hanging on to one of the porch supports.

"My God! She's talking!"

Jay jumped down, and the three of them sprinted toward the house.

Felipe Fernandez staggered out the door, holding a corner of his apron to a bleeding forehead.

"Stop him. Please, stop him!" Karen was sobbing.

"What happened?" Carlos yelled. "Did he hit you?"

Jay had Karen under the arms and was helping her to the porch chair. "No, no," she murmured. "Felipe tried to stop Daddy from leaving. Daddy hit him. And he threw me down."

Walker Hyde was examining the gash on the old cook's scalp, which was bleeding freely down his face.

"Karen, are you okay?" Jay asked.

"Yes, yes. Never mind about me. Did Daddy ride off?"

"Yes."

"You've got to stop him. He's going to kill someone."

"What? Who?"

"Some men. I don't know." She waved her hand irritably.

"Think! Did he say *where* he was going?" Carlos snapped.

The girl seemed to sag. She almost dissolved into tears. "No. He said something about taking care of his problem once and for all. Said he was going to shoot those men he'd bought those cattle from. Then he strapped on his gun and took his rifle and—"

"But he never mentioned any names or places?"

146

"No. Not that I remember. I had just awakened, and I heard a lot of commotion. He was arguing with Felipe."

"*Sí.* I tried to stop him, but he was wild. I try to hold him until he returned to his senses. But he struck me with the barrel of his gun. I have never seen Mr. Mac like this before."

"He took the road toward Patagonia," Jay said. "The same direction I was riding when Tige jumped me. Maybe we can catch him before he gets out of the hills."

Carlos shook his head. "I doubt it. By the time we get saddled he'll be gone too far to catch. That roan gelding of his is the fastest horse on this ranch. Besides, he could have circled around after he was out of sight. No telling which way he went."

Walker Hyde was on one knee beside the cook, wiping blood from the side of his face. He looked up suddenly. "You said he was going after the men who sold him these cattle. Carlos, did he ever say where these cattle came from? Did you know any o' those drovers who brought the first herd in here? Or the second?"

Carlos shook his head, frowning thoughtfully. Then his face brightened. "Jay! Remember when that herd passed us that night in the Santa Cruz Valley?"

Jay nodded.

"Remember when I heard some o' those drovers yelling to each other? That rider that came closest to us in the dark? Eddie and I recognized his voice as belonging to Billy Clanton, one of Old Man Clanton's sons."

"Yes, but what does that prove?"

"Nothing, really. But I'm sure they were rustling that herd out of Mexico. And if these sick cattle are out of Mexico, as the doc suspects, it's very likely they came from some of the rustled cattle the Clanton gang stole. Mr. Mac has to be riding to have it out with the Clantons. It's the only logical explanation."

"Let's go, then," Walker Hyde said. "Do you reckon

the boss is headed for their ranch house or to catch 'em in Tombstone, where they mostly hang out?''

"Let's try the ranch first," Carlos said. "It's on the San Pedro, not far from Tombstone. If he's not there, we'll head for town."

"Will you be all right here?" Jay asked Karen, with a solicitude in his voice that surprised even himself. "We're liable to be gone a day or two at least."

"I'll be fine," she replied, looking directly at him. "I've just got a terrible headache. I must have slept too hard or too long. I don't even remember coming back from my ride last night. I just don't remember." She looked around at the large herd grazing. "Did Daddy get all these cattle this morning?"

Jay smiled at her. She had come back to them. And her memory of those awful events was blank. She looked at him again. "Who are you? One of the new hands?"

"I'll tell you all about it later," Jay said, smiling again with great relief. He wanted to reach out and smooth her disheveled brunette hair back from that beautiful face that was slowly regaining its color. But he dared not. He was aware that the shock of her experience had caused her amnesia.

"C'mon, Jay. Felipe can take care of her," Carlos yelled, leaping off the porch and running toward the corral.

"Lightnin', get that Arabian out o' the barn. He's got better wind for a long run than some o' these others," Hyde said.

It was only a matter of minutes before their horses were caught and saddled. Jay ran into the bunkhouse and dug out the two extra boxes of .38-caliber cartridges for his Colt Lightning. In addition, he carried about twenty-five shells in his belt loops. Carlos had his six-gun, and Walker Hyde hooked the double-barreled shotgun over the saddle horn with a leather thong. Carlos quickly filled three big canteens from the ever-flowing iron spout, and they were ready to ride.

Jay waved to the girl, who still watched from the porch as the three of them swung into their saddles and spurred toward the upper end of the valley to take a cross-country route out of the Patagonias.

It lacked an hour of noon when they rode out of the small valley, Carlos leading the way.

They didn't stop for two hours. Alternately trotting and walking their horses, they covered several miles before pausing to dismount, stretch their legs, have a drink, and rest the horses. For the past hour they had been backtrailing the way they had come in the night before. Carlos and Walker used their hats to give the horses some water from their canteens, since there were no streams nearby. Even though they stood in the shade, they were all sweating from the closeness of the midday heat.

"We better decide what we gonna do when we get there," Walker Hyde said, shaking the remaining water out of his hat and putting it back on his head. "I seen that Clanton ranch house. It's built mostly like a fortress, with loopholes in those adobe walls. It sets up there on a hill above the river where they can see anybody comin' for miles. We jes gonna ride in there like we was invited kinfolk?"

"We got a while to think about it," Carlos replied. "We got a good long ride ahead of us yet. Probably won't get there before dark. The house is about twelve miles from Tombstone and about five miles this side of Charleston."

"We'd best get on, then," the black man said, reaching for his ground-reined horse.

They started out again, and Jay wondered about the wisdom of this course. He thought they probably should have ridden directly after McPherson in hopes of catching him. Even if the rancher had a good head start on them, they might be able to spot him once they were down out of the hills beyond Patagonia and on the flatter road north. This way they might miss him entirely, if Carlos had guessed wrong about where McPherson was headed. For all anyone knew, he might have been going no farther than Harshaw or Patagonia.

But he did not voice his doubts, and he gradually put them out of his mind as the afternoon wore on. He was amazed at the ground-eating pace they kept without tiring out the horses. The sun was still high when they came down out of the Huachucas into a broad valley on the eastern side. Here they stopped again to water the horses at a small stream and to relieve their cramped legs.

Jay swigged a few swallows from his canteen. They had to get to Clyde McPherson before someone was killed. He hoped they had guessed right. He capped the canteen and hung it back on the saddle horn. The horses were ripping up mouthfuls of grass from along the stream bank. Jay was tired and hungry, and he knew his companions were also. They silently mounted and started again.

Just at dusk they finally struck the San Pedro River. They turned their tired horses and followed its banks, thick-bordered with willows, sycamores, and big cottonwoods. After about a mile they spotted the Clanton ranch house on a broad, prominent hilltop across the river. As they drew closer, the words of Walker Hyde came back to Jay. The adobe walls did indeed resemble a fortress. There was no way they could go storming in there. In fact, they might already have been spotted, although there was no sign of life about the place that he could see from this distance. Maybe nobody was home. If McPherson had already beat them here and found no one home, he could have headed for Tombstone. Jay's heart rose a little at the thought. But his reason told him the rancher had not yet arrived, if he was coming this way at all. They would have spotted each other on the broad valley within the past two hours, more than likely.

Jay looked up toward the house again. The low adobe walls were catching the last high rays of the setting sun. He saw a slight movement. Several saddle horses were tethered on the far side of the house. His stomach tensed.

Carlos held up his hand, and the three of them reined up and dismounted. The horses immediately went for the water.

"He's not here yet," Carlos said, staring intently through the foliage at the horses about a half mile away. "The roan's not up there."

"It'll be dark soon," Walker said. "Do we wait or go on to Tombstone? The horses be about played out."

No one spoke for a few seconds.

"If we's gonna wait, we better yank the saddles off and let 'em roll and rest some," Walker added.

Jay offered no advice, since he was the newcomer here and he felt the other two knew Clyde McPherson a lot better than he did. It was the first time he had seen Carlos the least bit indecisive. Guaderrama took off his hat and wearily rubbed a hand over his face.

But then the decision was made for them.

"There's a rider!" Jay pointed through the trees at a trail of dust as a horse cantered up the long hillside toward the adobe house.

"That's Mr. Mac," Hyde said.

"Let's go," Carlos said.

Jay's hand went to the butt of his gun to make sure it was still securely in its holster as he mounted. He had checked it earlier to make sure it was loaded and working smoothly.

They urged their mounts down the bank into the current of the river. Jay caught his breath as the cold water soaked his legs. The river was about four feet deep here and about twenty yards wide.

Even as their horses lunged, streaming, out of the water, Jay knew they would never be able to head off the rancher before he reached the house. Jay measured the angle between them with his eye in the gathering dusk. And he knew for sure when he tried to kick the Arabian into a gallop up the slope. His mount just didn't have enough left to run. The horse took a few steps and faltered.

"Come on!" he yelled to the others. "Leave 'em here. They're too tired to wander off." He leapt to the ground and started to run up the incline toward the house. Carlos and Walker followed.

After riding most of the day, it felt good to stretch his legs in a good run.

If McPherson saw them in the deepening dusk, he gave no sign of it. While Jay was still a good quarter mile away, the rancher reached the house, leapt off his mount, and kicked the wooden door open.

Jay sprinted harder in his wet moccasins, slipping on the grass, his breathing deepening as the hill steepened.

When he was still a hundred yards from the house he heard the crash of muffled gunfire. Two shots, then three more in quick succession. Jay heard the crash of splintering furniture, a yell, and two more shots. He slowed as he approached the door and drew his Colt, waiting for Walker to come up with his shotgun.

"Oh, Lordy," the black man breathed behind him.

Jay was shaking, and it wasn't from the exertion.

"Hit the floor on each side when we go in," Carlos said. "Ready?"

They nodded.

"Now!"

Jay kicked open the door, which stood slightly ajar, and threw himself belly down and rolled to the left, gun forward and ready. Walker was on his heels and went the other way. Carlos was flat in the doorway, gun in hand.

A deafening roar blasted Jay's ears as a gun exploded in the room. A tongue of flame lashed toward the door. Two figures were moving on the far side of the room. The only light in the room was from the blazing coal-oil of a lamp that lay smashed on the floor.

Jay scuttled behind an overturned table. Another shot boomed, and a slug tore into the wood beside his head. As his eyes adjusted to the dim light, Jay squeezed off two shots. Then the shotgun roared and a body slammed back against the far wall. A man screamed.

"No more! No more! For God's sake, don't shoot any more. I give up."

Jay heard a pistol clatter to the floor. Then it got deathly quiet in the room. Powder smoke was thick and choking.

"Carlos! Are you all right?" Jay finally said, keeping his head close to the floor to breathe the cleaner air.

"Yes."

"Walker?"

"I'm here, Lightnin'. I reckon this gentleman has had enough fightin'."

Jay peered carefully around the edge of the table, Colt held cocked and ready. Walker Hyde held the shotgun on the one man in the room who remained standing.

Jay and Carlos slowly got to their feet. The air from the open window and door was slowly stirring and clearing the room of powder smoke. The rivulet of coal-oil still burned on the hard-packed dirt floor. A deck of playing cards lay scattered about. In the eerie, flickering light Jay saw a man backed against the far wall, his hands in the air. Three bodies were on the floor. One lay slumped on his back against the wall where Walker Hyde had shot him. Another was facedown, almost in the fire, Colt still clutched in his right hand. The back of his leather vest was stained with fresh blood.

Jay stepped around the table. On his back behind the table lay Clyde McPherson, the front of his white shirt reddened by a great loss of blood. Jay, his heart sinking, quickly knelt beside his boss and felt his throat for a pulse. There was none. Jay stood up and holstered his gun.

"He's dead." There was a catch in his voice, and he cleared his throat. He saw the stunned looks on their faces. "We did everything we could to head this off, boys," he said, his throat still feeling tight.

Carlos and Walker said nothing.

"Is there anyone else in the house?" Jay demanded of the cowboy who stood with his hands up.

"No. Who the hell are you, any—"

"Shut up!" Hyde snapped. His hands, holding the 12-gauge, were shaking.

"Carlos, better see if there's a wagon out back we can hitch up. We're going into town," Jay said, taking charge, since the others seemed to be still in shock.

Carlos disappeared out the door.

"I'll keep this one covered, if you want to help him," Jay said to Hyde. The black man nodded and handed over the shotgun. Jay saw tears glistening in the older man's eyes as he glanced toward the body of Clyde McPherson.

Jay swallowed hard. His mouth and throat were dry. He felt strange with so much death around him.

"Mister, can I put my hands down? I won't make no moves. I been hit."

"Okay." Jay nodded.

The cowboy let his hands down slowly to his sides, and Jay noted the trickles of blood dripping off the man's left hand. There was a bloody spot on the arm of his shirt near the elbow.

Jay didn't speak as he waited. There would be time for questions and answers later.

In a few minutes, Jay heard the jangle of harness chain outside. He backed up and glanced out the doorway. Carlos and Walker had a buckboard drawn up in front.

The three bodies were carried out and laid in the back and covered with two blankets from the bedrooms. The prisoner rode on the seat with his hands tied to the iron handrail. Jay tied his Arabian to the tailgate and took up the reins to drive. Carlos and Walker also tied their horses behind the wagon and threw their saddles on two of the horses from the corral.

On the drive to town, Jay felt the weight of fatigue dragging at his body and mind. The hours of riding with no food, ending in the sudden gun battle, were taking their toll on him. The letdown was setting in as the adrenalin ebbed, and the shock of McPherson's death numbed him.

He automatically slapped the reins over the backs of the team to urge them up out of a sandy wash. The prisoner sat silently, leaning to his left, both hands tied to the slim iron handrail of the wooden buckboard seat, feet braced on the footboard against the jolting of the wagon.

Tired as he was, Jay realized that this might be his only chance to question this cowboy about McPherson's role in the scheme that had led to the shoot-out. Once they got to town and faced the questioning of the law in the form of Sheriff Behan, they might get no information at all, since Behan was a known protector of the cowboy faction and would make sure this man gave no incriminating statements. Maybe Jay could catch him off guard and get some information from him now.

"That arm bothering you much?" Jay asked, eyeing him sideways.

"Huh?" The man seemed somewhat dazed. "Yeah, it hurts like hell," he finally replied in a dull voice. "You can untie me; I ain't goin' nowheres."

"Sorry, but I can't watch you and drive at the same time," Jay replied easily.

The cowboy grunted and lapsed into silence. The slug had passed through his forearm, breaking no bone and apparently missing any arteries. But beyond that they could not tell what damage had been done. A strip torn from a tablecloth had served to bind the wound and staunch the bleeding.

The man's dull reaction indicated he might be in shock,

Jay thought—whether from loss of blood or the swiftness of the unexpected attack that had killed two of his friends, Jay couldn't know.

"We tried to get there in time to stop McPherson," Jay said. "But we didn't quite make it."

"Huh!" the man grunted, and spat off the side of the buckboard. "He didn't have no cause to bust in there, ravin' about some sick cattle we'd sold him. Hell, they weren't sick when we drove 'em up to his place." The cowboy twisted his head so he could look toward Jay in the dark. "Who the hell *are* you boys, anyway?"

"We worked for McPherson. What did McPherson say when he came in?"

"He accused us of us sellin' him rustled cattle that had foot-and-mouth disease, and then called us all kinds of foul names. Raul wasn't havin' none o' that and yanked his gun and they went to blazin' away. Then Joe and I got into it, and then you busted in."

"Where'd you get those Mexican cattle you sold him?" Jay asked.

"We didn't rustle 'em, if that's what you're gettin' at," the man replied guardedly. "Billy and the boys got legal bills o' sale for 'em and everything."

"I'll bet if we went and talked to someone on the Verdugo spread we'd get a different tale. Anybody can make up bogus bills of sale."

"Can't you loosen these ropes?" the man groaned. "My arm's painin' me somethin' fierce."

Jay ignored the plea and kept his eyes ahead. The clopping of the horses' hooves was loud on the hard-packed road.

"Why was McPherson buying cattle from the Clanton outfit?"

"How should I know?" The man winced as the buckboard hit a rut. "Hear tell he was startin' up a herd."

"Did he know where you got those cattle?"

156

"If you mean did he know they was Mexican, yeah, I guess so."

"Did he know they were rustled?"

"They wasn't stolen, I tell you. Billy had papers on 'em, and that's all McPherson wanted to see. He was mostly interested in two good bulls we had in that last bunch he bought."

It seemed really incredible, Jay thought, that a man could get so enraged over a herd he was losing to disease that he would go for these men with blood in his eye. But then, McPherson was in the position of losing thousands of dollars—maybe facing financial ruin as a result. And maybe he had ridden to the Clanton place with the idea of talking tough and threatening them unless they returned his money. But he apparently had goaded them too far, and the cowboy named Raul had gone for his gun.

"Why didn't McPherson talk to Billy or Ike Clanton, instead of you three?" Jay asked.

"They wasn't there. They'd gone down to Charleston to meet the McLaureys and have a few drinks. That made McPherson even madder when we told him they was gone. He was just loaded for bear, and we was handy. That crazy sonuvabitch. I'm glad we got him."

Jay felt a flare of temper at this remark but held his tongue. Three men were dead tonight, and there would be hell to pay later. No sense getting into an argument with this wounded cowboy.

They rolled into Tombstone at ten minutes to eleven. Jay pulled the buckboard to a stop in front of the brightly lit windows of the Occidental Saloon. He stepped down and tied the team to the hitching rail.

"Be right back, boys," he said as Carlos and Walker sat their horses.

He returned in less than five minutes, followed closely by Burnett. "I sent one of the loafers to roust Doc Goodfellow out of bed," Burnett announced. "He'll be down shortly. You boys want to step down and come in for a drink while you're waiting?''

Carlos shook his head. "We'll get this business over with first.''

Burnett nodded. "I understand.''

Jay introduced his two companions to Burnett. Except for a black left eye and some swelling over the bridge of his nose the big man looked none the worse for his marathon bout with the miner.

"See you back down here later?'' the bartender asked Jay as he turned to go back inside. "I want to hear the whole story.''

Jay nodded.

Dr. Goodfellow turned up about fifteen minutes later, sleepy-eyed, and with his shirttail hanging outside his pants.

"What the hell happened here?'' he demanded gruffly as he dismounted. The ten-gallon hat he wore partially made up for his lack of height. He sported a huge walrus mustache that gave him almost a comical appearance. But the doc was not one to be tampered with. He had been a boxer in his youth.

He directed them to haul the bodies to the undertaker's, where he helped carry them inside and laid them on the tables. He examined them briefly before leaving and locking the door behind him. From there they all proceeded to the doctor's office, where he treated the wounded cowboy's arm.

The cowboy, who gave his name as Jim Hughes, at first stated that Clyde McPherson attacked them with no reason. But with the arrival of Sheriff Behan and one of his deputies, the man finally admitted that McPherson had accused them of forcing him to buy rustled cattle from Mexico that had foot-and-mouth disease. But Hughes insisted that he was just a hired hand and knew nothing about any rustling. He swore that Billy and Ike Clanton had produced bills of sale to McPherson for all cattle sold to the rancher.

"Sheriff, I'd bet you a handful of double eagles that those cattle on McPherson's place were stolen from the Verdugo spread in northern Sonora," Carlos said. "It wouldn't take but a few days to fetch the owner or the foreman up here to identify them and testify that those cattle were never sold; they were stolen. And I have a hunch they'd testify they know who did it, too."

"It's a lie!"

"We'll see about that later," Sheriff Behan said. "If you've got that arm patched up, Doc, I'll have my deputy lock him up over at the jail. I'll see about him tomorrow. And I'm gonna lock up this black man for murderin' one of those boys with a shotgun. I oughta lock up the whole bunch o' ya while I get this sorted out," he added.

"You're not lockin' up Walker Hyde," Carlos said grimly. "We'll be in town so you can find us, but he's not goin' into your jail."

The sheriff went pale, but he saw that he and his deputy were outgunned by the three men who stood around them.

"If it'll make you feel any better, I'll put all of us in the protective custody of the town marshal, Virgil Earp, until the coroner's inquest is held."

"Fair enough. I'll send for him." Behan looked almost relieved to save face without a confrontation.

While waiting for the marshal, Behan sent his deputy to stable the horses.

Virgil Earp, a muscular six-footer with a round face and sporting a thick mustache and a black suit, showed up a few minutes later. When apprised of the situation, he said, "Good. I'll assign one man to stay with you until the coroner's inquest. Probably tomorrow afternoon." Earp seemed pleasant enough, but competent and businesslike. Jay felt much more comfortable with this man than he did with Behan.

"Hell, Sheriff, why're you lockin' me up if you're lettin' them run loose?" the cowboy objected as Dr. Goodfellow finished bandaging the man's arm wound. "Hell, *I* was the one who was attacked. I was just defendin' myself."

Behan hesitated. "Okay. You're free to go until the inquest. Just be sure to stay in town."

"Nothin' could get me back out to that ranch house," Hughes said, and almost bolted out the office door, his arm in a sling. He headed straight for the Oriental Saloon down the street.

"That'll be the last anyone sees of that man," Carlos remarked quietly to Jay and Walker as the three of them left the doctor's office and crossed the street toward the Occidental. "He'll have a few drinks with his friends, borrow or steal a horse, and head for parts unknown."

It was half past midnight when the trio finally sat down at a corner table to rest and eat after fasting for more than twenty-four hours. Burnett turned his bartending duties over to another man and came to join them, bringing them generous slices of yellow cheese from the bar, dill pickles, foaming mugs of beer, a loaf of brown bread, and thick slices of ham.

Around mouthfuls of food they related the story from the time they had left Tombstone almost thirty-six hours before.

Burnett whistled softly. "Damn! Too bad McPherson was killed. I didn't know the man, but maybe his testimony could have put the whole Clanton outfit away for good."

"Two of them have been put away for good tonight," Jay replied, keeping his voice low and glancing around. The man Earp had assigned to watch them sat discreetly out of earshot, playing a game of solitaire and sipping a beer.

"It's going to be awfully hard to break the news to

160

Karen," Jay said, thinking of the anguished look on that beautiful face as they had ridden away.

Carlos nodded. "She's just gotten over one bad shock. I hope this doesn't send her off again."

"Pretty tough finding out your father's in league with the worst rustlers in the territory, and then shot dead by them at the same time."

"Maybe that little missy can stand it better than the shame of having her daddy sent to prison," Hyde remarked.

They discussed the night's events for a while longer. When the clock on a shelf above the back bar chimed one-thirty, Jay scrubbed a hand across his bearded face and stifled a yawn. "I've got to get to bed, gents. That food was just what I needed to put me away for about ten hours."

The three of them got up, bade Burnett good-night, and headed for the Grand Hotel.

# CHAPTER 19

**F**RESHLY bathed and shaved, Jay, Walker, and Carlos sat at breakfast in the Can-Can Restaurant the next morning at ten. Virgil Earp's deputy was nowhere to be seen, but Jay guessed he was somewhere close by.

Jay felt clean, rested, and almost relaxed after the grueling two days they had just spent. They were halfway through a large helping of fried eggs and fried potatoes when Burnett swung his bulk into the dining room. He was looking a little tired, but his handlebar mustache was freshly waxed.

"Just got some news from George McIntosh over at the Western Union office you might be interested in," he said, pulling up a chair and nodding his thanks for a cup of coffee Walker Hyde poured for him.

"What's that?"

"Word just came from over in the Animas Valley in New Mexico that Old Man Clanton and several of his men—Dick Gray, Bud Snow, Harry Ernshaw, Billy Lang, and Jim Crane—were all ambushed and killed by some Mexicans a few days ago."

"What?"

"That's right. Supposedly, they were driving a herd of stolen Mexican beef from Clanton's ranch to Tombstone to

162

sell them. They were coming by way of Guadalupe Canyon, just across the Mexican line. They had stopped to camp there overnight and were ambushed and every last one of them shot. No witnesses left, but they're assumin' it was the Mexicans they had stolen the herd from."

They all glanced at one another.

"Well, it looks like the Clanton gang is being whittled away little by little," Carlos finally said. "There won't be much left for Behan and the Earps to fight about before long."

"Don't you believe it," Burnett said, shaking his head. "This thing between the Earp and Behan crowds is festerin' up like a boil, a political feud that's been building for months. I'm guessin' it won't be long before it bursts. And since you and McPherson killed two of the Clanton gang, it looks like you may have thrown in on the side of the Earps, like it or not."

They finished eating and paid the waitress for their meal. Just as they all stood up to leave, Jay spotted Sheriff Dawson of Washington Camp and his nephew, Tige, coming in the door. This time Jay saw Tige first and his hand dropped to the butt of his Colt as he edged away from the others. Walker Hyde saw them too, and he slipped Carlos's gun from its holster.

Then Tige looked up and spotted Jay. He stopped in his tracks. Tige saw one gun covering him and Jay's hand on his Colt. Tige's eyes flickered at the others, then he dropped his gaze and walked on past them toward a table.

"Put that damn gun away, nigger," Sheriff Dawson said to Hyde. "We don't want any trouble here."

Jay was amazed. He could only stare at his adversary, who had been hounding him for weeks.

The pair seated themselves while Jay and the others continued to stare.

"Go on about your business, son," Sheriff Dawson said, looking up.

"You don't want me?" Jay finally managed to articulate.

"About the shooting of that Mexican kid? No. Tige didn't tell you?"

"Tell me what?"

"We found a slug buried in a post right where the boy was standing. It was a .45-caliber, not a .38. It could have been the one that got him. We'll never know. In any case, Judge Nicholson dismissed the charge for lack of evidence. Technically, you're still a fugitive for bustin' outa my jail. But I may be inclined to look the other way if you get the hell outa the territory."

A wave of relief swept over Jay, but he forced himself to look belligerent. "What about my six hundred dollars you took from me when you locked me up?" he asked, approaching the table.

The sheriff looked up and eyed him carefully. "Don't push your luck, sonny."

Jay stared into the hard eyes of the lawman for a few seconds and then turned and walked out. In spite of the money loss, he felt as if a great weight had been lifted from him. He could not even feel sad when he suddenly saw Karen McPherson and Felipe Fernandez come out of the undertaker's parlor and start toward them down the sidewalk.

When she saw them she burst into tears and covered her face with her hands. Carlos went up and put his arms around her. She was wearing a riding skirt and boots, so Jay guessed she and Felipe had ridden into Tombstone either late last night or early this morning without knowing about Clyde McPherson's death.

They all turned to walk along together. Walker Hyde fell in beside the old Mexican cook and briefly explained what had happened. Jay could hear Carlos, a trusted friend of Karen's, quietly telling her of the disaster. Jay noted that Carlos was careful to omit the gruesome details of the shoot-out.

164

By the time they reached the end of the street and stepped off the boardwalk into the sunshine of the dusty street, Karen had regained her composure. She wiped her eyes with a bandanna and raked her fingers through her dark hair, pushing it back from her face. "I'd swear my father didn't know those cattle were stolen. He mentioned to me several times that he wanted to get a herd started but was short of cash. He didn't much like dealing with the Clantons because of their reputation, but I guess he took a chance and accepted their bills of sale because the price wasn't too high. Whatever wrong my father did, he's more than paid for it now. I loved him. I'll always remember him for the good man he was."

So there it was. A good man gone bad, or a naive man who chose to ignore the warning signs that all was not right and clear with the beef cattle he was purchasing. Jay didn't know, and McPherson would never be able to tell his side of the story. Had he been duped into buying cattle at bargain prices, thinking that the price was right because most of them were not top-quality animals? Jay made up his mind that this was the case. He would never allow himself to think ill of the man who had been so kind to him. And he had a gut feeling that the others would act that way toward Karen McPherson, regardless of any doubts they might harbor deep in their hearts.

"Miz McPherson, if you need me to stay on and help you at the ranch, I'd be mos' happy to," Walker Hyde said.

"That goes for me, too," Carlos said. "I don't know about Eddie Flynn."

"I thank you all," she replied. "But I'm going to take things one step at a time from now on. The first thing I need to do is see to my poor father's funeral. Then we have to deal with those cattle. I understand they must all be destroyed. That will be a big job, and I'll need your help. We have to cooperate with the authorities to stop the spread of this terrible disease. I'm not sure yet how I'll pay you. Maybe I can sell the ranch and pay you. I haven't had time to think about all that. Daddy had a will, I think, but I don't know what it says. I'll have to find my brother.'' Tears glistened in her eyes again.

She turned to seek out Jay. "You're looking a lot better than you did last time I saw you," she said with a trace of a smile. "At least you shaved and seem a lot cleaner. Felipe tells me I owe you a great debt. You risked your life to save me from the Apaches. I'll admit I have absolutely no recollection of that.'' She slipped her arm in his as they started walking again. "Maybe you can take the time to tell me all about it later," she said, squinting up at him in the sunlight.

"Yes," Jay answered, a little flustered. "Yes, we'll have plenty of time later."

**Tim Champlin**, born John Michael Champlin in Fargo, North Dakota, was graduated from Middle Tennessee State University and earned a Master's degree from Peabody College in Nashville, Tennessee. Beginning his career as an author of the Western story with *Summer of the Sioux* in 1982, the American West represents for him "a huge, ever-changing block of space and time in which an individual had more freedom than the average person has today . . . For those brave, and sometimes desperate souls who ventured West looking for a better life, it must have been an exciting time to be alive." Champlin has achieved a notable stature in being able to capture that time in complex, often exciting, and historically accurate fictional narratives. He is the author of two series of Western novels, that concerned with Matt Tierney who comes of age in *Summer of the Sioux* and who begins his professional career as a reporter for the Chicago *Times-Herald* covering an expeditionary force venturing into the Big Horn country and the Yellowstone, and Jay McGraw, a callow youth who is plunged into outlawry at the beginning of *Colt Lightning*. There are six books in the Matt Tierney series and with *Deadly Season* a fifth featuring Jay McGraw. In all of Champlin's stories there are always unconventional plot ingredients, striking historical details, vivid characterizations of the multitude of ethnic and cultural diversity found on the frontier, and narratives rich and original and surprising. His exuberant tapestries include lumber schooners sailing the West Coast, early-day wet-plate photography, daredevils who thrill crowds with gas balloons and the first parachutes, Tong Wars in San Francisco's Chinatown, Basque sheepherders, and the Penitentes of the Southwest, and are always highly entertaining. *Swift Thunder* is his latest title.